D1240688

SPECIAL MESSAGE TO READERS

This book is published under the auspices of

THE ULVERSCROFT FOUNDATION

(registered charity No. 264873 UK)

Established in 1972 to provide funds for research, diagnosis and treatment of eye diseases. Examples of contributions made are: —

A Children's Assessment Unit at Moorfield's Hospital, London.

•

Twin operating theatres at the Western Ophthalmic Hospital, London.

•

A Chair of Ophthalmology at the Royal Australian College of Ophthalmologists.

•

The Ulverscroft Children's Eye Unit at the Great Ormond Street Hospital For Sick Children, London.

You can help further the work of the Foundation by making a donation or leaving a legacy. Every contribution, no matter how small, is received with gratitude. Please write for details to:

THE ULVERSCROFT FOUNDATION,
The Green, Bradgate Road, Anstey,
Leicester LE7 7FU, England.
Telephone: (0116) 236 4325

In Australia write to:

THE ULVERSCROFT FOUNDATION,
c/o The Royal Australian and New Zealand
College of Ophthalmologists,
94-98 Chalmers Street, Surry Hills,
N.S.W. 2010, Australia

THE SECRET FILES OF SHERLOCK HOLMES

The Adventure of the Missing Detective: Whilst travelling incognito in Switzerland, Sherlock Holmes is shocked almost beyond belief to discover that Queen Victoria is dead — and that his old nemesis, Professor James Moriarty, had not only survived their confrontation at the Reichenbach Falls, but had been knighted and appointed personal advisor to the new heir! Meanwhile, *The American Adventure* provides a fascinating insight into Holmes' earlier life when, during his travels with Dr. Joseph Bell, he was tutored in the art of deduction by the master . . .

Books by E. C. Tubb
in the Linford Mystery Library:

SHERLOCK HOLMES AND THE
CROSBY MURDERS

GARY LOVISI

THE SECRET FILES OF SHERLOCK HOLMES

Complete and Unabridged

LINFORD
Leicester

First published in Great Britain

First Linford Edition
published 2009

British Library CIP Data

Lovisi, Gary.
The secret files of Sherlock Holmes - -
(Linford mystery library)
1. Holmes, Sherlock (Fictitious character)
- -Fiction. 2. Detective and mystery stories,
American. 3. Large type books.
I. Title II. Series III. Lovisi, Gary. Adventure
of the missing detective. IV. Lovisi, Gary.
American adventure.
813.5′4–dc22

ISBN 978–1–84782–828–6

Published by
F. A. Thorpe (Publishing)
Anstey, Leicestershire

Set by Words & Graphics Ltd.
Anstey, Leicestershire
Printed and bound in Great Britain by
T. J. International Ltd., Padstow, Cornwall

This book is printed on acid-free paper

The Adventure of the Missing Detective

Here is a strange tale for you, gentle reader, one that is perhaps the most fantastic adventure of Sherlock Holmes' entire career. I have left it for posterity, secreted with my special papers at Cox & Co., to be opened in the future, and done with as my heirs deem best.

Here now are the circumstances of that story as I heard them from Holmes' own lips . . .

⋆ ⋆ ⋆

As you know, Watson, my return to London after the happenings at the Reichenbach Falls was not in 1894 as you have written in your amusing account of the Moran case for the popular press. I will relate to you now the actual story of what occurred during those missing years when you, and the world, thought me dead.

It was during the affair at Reichenbach. Moriarty was dead, destroyed by the furious power of the Reichenbach Falls. I had seen his body dashed to the jagged rocks below. I had seen his head crushed on those very same rocks. Then I had unaccountably lost my own balance, taken by some strange sudden draft of wind, no doubt, which caused me to plummet into a mysterious vortex of whirling fog and roiling mists below. It was a cold and supercharged atmosphere that I entered, quite unlike anything I had ever experienced before. My fall seemed to descend almost in stages, slowly, staggered, even sluggish. I could not comprehend it at all. It was a most unnatural affair, and nothing at all in the manner of which the Professor met his timely demise barely minutes before. My descent was somewhat transcendental in nature. It may have even been miraculous, for it was unusual in the extreme and seemed to bypass what I know of our laws of physics and gravity.

That final encounter with Moriarty, and my resulting injury, had caused a long convalescence. If not for the kind ministrations of an isolated hill folk couple, I surely would have passed on from a comatose state to death. As it was, I spent much time in that near-death dream state, lost in a miasma of thoughts, my mind playing tricks, nightmares wracking my brain, even as my body lay still and silent in an apparent total vegetative existence.

After some time, I came out of my coma, and as I slowly recuperated, was eventually well enough to question my Swiss rescuers. As you can well imagine, I had many questions. Hans and Gerda were a simple farm couple who had a small parcel of land below Interlaken. They told me of how Hans had found me at the bottom of a lonely ravine, apparently uninjured. Initially he thought I was merely asleep, but he soon discovered that I was in the grip of some deliberative state and summoning Gerda, the couple took me into their small cabin to care for me.

Once I regained consciousness I found I had lost much weight and was extremely weak. After I had regained some strength, I listened with great interest to Hans' and Gerda's story. I did not tell them about Moriarty or my tumult over the ledge near the Great Falls. That would have seemed incongruous with the fact that the few minor bruises I had sustained were much too insignificant injuries for one who had gone through such a violent fall. It did not make sense, but you will see that this was just the beginning of a series of incidents and activities that made little sense to me at the time, but by the end of this strange narrative will all be explained.

In fact, quite early on I began to believe there might be a more significant mystery here than met the eye. You see, just as Moriarty met his death from going over the falls — and I saw him with my own eyes meet his doom before I myself plunged downward — I also should have been killed from my own incredible fall. However, there was something about that mist, the wind, perhaps various air currents and updrafts? I do not know for certain, but something saved me and seemingly with great gentility set me down upon the lush green sward of the ravine bottom where Hans later found me.

I make no explanation for it at all. I cannot explain the lack of injury or my comatose state. I am no man of science, save where the criminal element is concerned. Perhaps my friend the distinguished Professor Challenger would make something more of it. Suffice it to say that I was at least satisfied with the results of the situation. Moriarty was dead and I was alive.

Before I left the area below Interlaken, I asked my kind hosts if they or those in the nearby village remembered anyone having come around looking for me. I also asked them if any tourist had gone missing, or if there were reports of anyone killed in an accident off the falls. Hans and Gerda told me they had no such knowledge, but when I told Hans to ask around the village, he returned with interesting news indeed. While I was apparently not missed at all, it appears an

Englishman, perhaps on holiday at the time, had in fact died going over the falls on the very same day that I had my own descent. I was told the body had been claimed and was buried in the local cemetery by a visitor friend from London.

I sighed with relief. Moriarty, no doubt. I only thought it strange that you, good Watson, or my brother, Mycroft, had not yet found me.

Months later as I took my leave from Hans and Gerda I decided to book a small room at an inn of the lower village for a few days. It was a robust little place, one of those lively alpine respites, and I began to feel more in tune with the world I had been so long estranged from since my injury. Hans and Gerda, the souls of propriety and generosity lived a private and lonely life in a secluded area. Now I was back in a village among people and activity and beginning to get back to my old self again. Why, I was even able to find an English newspaper to catch up with events in the world and back home. It was a copy of the *London Times* and I began to peruse it nonchalantly.

It felt good to feel the *Times* in my hands again, to smell the newsprint, to see the well-remembered large lettering of the headlines and the many narrow columns of small and tightly packed print for the various news items from all around the world.

However, one item below the fold caught my attention as no other has in my life. I read it with shock and dismay. The horror I felt, the alarm and confusion was something I had never experienced before. I grew dizzy, weak-kneed, my heart raced. I read it once again, very carefully. The news item was rather simple and matter-of-fact. In essence it said this: *The British Monarch, King Albert Christian Edward Victor, former Duke of Clarence and Avondale, and grandson of the late Queen Victoria, will bestow the honour of a knighthood upon Mr. James Moriarty. The well-known and respected Professor of Mathematics, formerly at one of our most prestigious universities, is the author of various noted scientific works, including, 'The Dynamics of An Asteroid,' which has been well-received in academic circles. He is being honoured for his invaluable service to the Crown. The ceremony is to take place upon the 24th day of April in the year of Our Lord 1892, at Buckingham Palace.*

I thought this must be some bizarre type of joke or even a misprint, or perhaps suddenly I had become deranged and entirely lost my mind from my injury. Victoria, dead? Eddy, the new king! Why, was it not rumored in dark circles, that he was under suspicion in the Ripper murders? But more so, Moriarty, *alive!* It was incomprehensible! I had seen him die! His body had been buried. Now, if this news item was to be believed, he was not only alive, but to receive a knighthood of all things! It was preposterous, outrageous, and the news left me totally astonished, perplexed and nonplussed. Yet it gave me much food for thought, and it was food that would *not* stay down.

Immediately I perused that newspaper closely from front to back. It was a chilling experience, let me tell you, my friend. The brunt of it all seems to be that it appears as if the entire world I have known all my life had gone irrevocably and incomprehensibly mad. All was upside down and *wrong!*

Here then, is some of what I gleaned from my perusal of that one issue. Our Gracious Majesty, Queen Victoria was, in fact, dead, as was her son and heir, Edward. I found an article that spoke of a Court of Inquiry which had recently cleared their deaths of any but natural causes in a carriage accident, even though rumours and questions apparently abounded that it had been no accident at all! No autopsy had been performed upon the royal personages. A disturbing turn of events under the circumstances. In other areas news items leaped out at me and they were the most incongruous with the facts that I knew. One of the most bizarre was that a military dictatorship was assuming control in the United States and that there was the threatened succession of five western states from the Union. It appeared to be civil war all over again. Russia was in turmoil, the government of France had fallen, and a united Germany had suddenly risen from the ashes of Bismarck's

Prussia and appeared to be making ready for world war.

There was more, but I'll not bore you with the details of the many seemingly trivial items that in and of themselves appeared insignificant, but to my trained eyes and historical knowledge were no less disturbing and fantastic by their very existence.

Something very big and far afield was happening throughout the world. Things were very wrong. I could not fathom it, but if I did not know better, I would be pressed to admit that this might be some trick, set into motion by Moriarty. A fantastic thought, surely, and utterly unfounded, for he was dead. Nevertheless, while logic told me what was true, my intuition told me differently. You know I seldom listen to emotions; they are not to be trusted in my line of work. Nevertheless, one question nagged my thoughts. That newspaper said Moriarty was alive. How could that be? How could Moriarty be *alive* — and have been knighted — when I *knew* he was dead?

A chilling thought suddenly grabbed

me — could it have been someone else entirely who plummeted over the falls? Someone disguised as Moriarty? Even as I considered the thought I knew it just could not be possible, nevertheless some investigation seemed warranted.

Now I knew that I must seek out that grave here in the village and determine that which was within.

⋆ ⋆ ⋆

The next night was cloudy and moonless, an alpine version of those evenings you may remember that shrouded the moors around Baskerville Hall so many years ago in dire gloom. It was the perfect evening for the dark business I had that night with my nemesis — who now seemingly dogged me in death, even as he had in life.

I enlisted the help of good Hans in my nocturnal investigation, telling him just enough to let him know how important it was for me to see the body in that coffin. He was somewhat concerned about such activities, but being a former medical student, agreed to help when I made clear it was important to me.

Now I had to be sure that Moriarty's casket held *his* body!

* * *

It was after midnight and the village was wrapped up tightly for the evening as Hans and I stole out of the back door of my little inn and he lead me to the small cemetery on the outskirts of the village.

We quietly walked through a carved wooden arch, and entered a small fenced-in area of burial plots topped with memorials and statues in stone and wood. Hans brought me to one such lonely grave at an isolated spot in the end. The marker was a simple wooden cross, its inscription Hans translated for me.

'It says, 'English Man, Died, May 1891',' Hans whispered.

I nodded. I looked around us carefully. There was no one. All was quiet and peaceful. Hans and I began to dig.

I cannot express to you the excitement that surged through me as my spade cut into the hard cold earth, and once it finally hit the lid of the pine box that contained that with which I was seeking.

Now was the moment of truth. Hans and I quickly cleared away the last of the dirt so as to make the top of the plain wooden casket accessible. Hans looked at me and I nodded, then he began using a crow bar to pry open the casket.

With a loud screeching of rusted nails, the lid finally came off and we saw that a tall male body wrapped in shrouds lay before us. I motioned Hans away. I quickly knelt down before the corpse. Deftly, I removed the shroud cloths, until I had a full view of the face.

There had been some decay and natural parasite activity upon the flesh of the face, but the cold climate ensured there was more than enough left for me to make a very definite determination. I froze with astonishment and some fear, my blood ran cold, for the face I now looked upon was not that of Professor James Moriarty at all. It was the face of Sherlock Holmes! It was my very own face!

Hans asked me if everything was all right. He said that I did not look well. Hans would not look closely at the face of the corpse, while I could not take my eyes away from it. You can imagine my reaction. I hardly knew what to make of this at all. At first I thought it might be some trick or joke. I was here after all, and alive, was I not?

You know my methods and I never theorize before I obtain all the facts. I have said so over and over again, that solving cases is a matter of eliminating the impossible — and then whatever remains, however improbable, must be the truth. I felt that what I was viewing now created implications that would soon test that maxim to the very limit. You see, that corpse before me bore silent witness to the truth of this strange event and I vowed it would tell me all it knew before this dark night was over.

'Hans,' I ordered. 'Bring that lantern closer, I must examine the body.'

Then I began what can only be described as a very methodical and detailed search of the corpse to rule out all suppositions until I could get to the truth of this matter.

What I discovered was even more bizarre and shocking than anything you could have ever put into your little accounts of my cases for the popular press. First of all, the corpse was that of an actual human being, not any statue or manikin. By all accounts the man appeared to have met his death sometime within the last year. There were severe bruises and a few broken bones from his fall that I immediately noticed. However, it was the physical characteristics that were interesting to me in the extreme. The corpse appeared to be my age, my height, my weight, wore my own clothing, and had my exact physical appearance in every category. I was shocked and dismayed. Needless to say I examined the body as detailed as possible under the lantern light held so steadily by my trusty Hans. And the more I looked, the more I could only come up with one determination. It was me! There was no doubt. I even examined the sole of the right foot of the corpse. There I found the scar, an exact duplicate of which was on my own right foot. I had acquired it as a young boy. No one but Mycroft and I knew of it. I tell you, it was uncanny. The corpse was not just someone who looked like me, or was made up to look like me. It was not some copy, but an original. It was me! I was looking upon the dead body of Sherlock Holmes!

This was a discovery that set my world reeling in more ways than one. It allowed, even demanded, that my thoughts now entertain a multitude of questions that I had hitherto ignored. Surely something mysterious had befallen me at the Reichenbach. That mist, my fall, the coma, now it began to make some sense. But what indeed, did it portend? Something strange, no doubt, perhaps supernatural. The very thought surprised me greatly.

Although perplexed at this discovery and the questions it raised, I had to put them all aside. For all I knew for certain now was this: with Moriarty apparently alive, I must get home to London, immediately.

For I was sure everyone I knew there was in great danger. The world I knew did not exist any longer, and somehow I was in a new world, or a different, perhaps alternate one. Here I had died at the Reichenbach, while Moriarty had somehow lived and has been free to make his plans and schemes.

I feared for Mycroft now.

I feared for you, Watson.

I feared for England, the Empire — the world.

⋆ ⋆ ⋆

The boat train took me into Victoria Station in London's centre on schedule as always. I noticed the familiar building but it was now draped with black sashes and bunting in mourning and remembrance of our dear deceased queen. It was a sombre homecoming.

I was in disguise as an old sailor. I knew it would be best to get the lay of the land, so to speak, and then decide on a course of action before I made my presence known.

Quite honestly at that moment, I was not sure what to do. For the first time in my life I was far out of my depths, but I knew there was one sure anchor in my world, or worlds, and that was you, good Watson, and our rooms at 221B. So I headed for Baker Street, an apparent elderly sailor on pension, a bit taken with drink and fallen on hard times. That latter part of my disguise was more true than I'd have cared to admit.

Baker Street came into view and appeared the same as always, but as I approached the building that housed 221B my heart sank and a great feeling of gloom overtook me. The building was closed and boarded up. It appeared a massive fire had gutted the entire structure many months back.

I ran to our lodgings and looked with disbelief at the boarded up building and then at the people passing by on the street, desperately seeking a friendly or recognizable face. Mrs. Hudson, Billy, Wiggins, anyone!

'My good man!' I shouted to a neighbour. 'Can you tell me what happened to this house and the people who lived here?'

'Aye, Pops,' he replied, shaking his head sadly. 'Not much to say, big fire last year, a real shame.'

'What of the doctor?' I asked.

'Oh the doctor? The doctor went off, no one knows where. The lady what owned the house I hear tell is living with a sister in Kent.'

I sighed with relief. At least you, and Mrs. Hudson, were alive. But where?

'And what of Mr. Sherlock Holmes?' I asked with more trepidation than I realized I possessed.

'Aye, the detective? Dead this past year. It broke the doctor's poor 'eart, I tell you.'

I nodded, feeling as if I was in a dream. Or a nightmare. This just could not be. I took one last look at the rooms we had shared for so long in happier days, and then went on my way.

* * *

I am afraid that I received even worse news at the Diogenes Club. After Baker

Street I immediately hailed a hansom cab and made my way to Pall Mall. There I entered that venerable establishment, only allowed into the environs of the Visitors Room, where I was informed by a liveried butler that Mr. Mycroft Holmes was no longer a member of the Diogenes Club.

'Why is that?' I asked, still in my disguise as the old retired sailor.

The butler looked at me with obvious annoyance from being asked to explain such things to one of the lower classes, but then shrugged and added, 'Murdered he was, last May, not soon after his famous brother died on holiday in Switzerland, I hear.'

'Assassinated,' I whispered. 'Oh, Mycroft, now I see . . . '

'Sir?' the butler inquired.

'Nothing,' I replied. 'I will be leaving now.'

* * *

On the street before the Diogenes Club I stood frozen, stunned, it surely seemed all was lost. Mycroft my brother, dead? Murdered? Murdered no doubt by Moriarty's henchmen no sooner he returned to London from the Reichenbach. Watson, you were gone. Where? The world in turmoil, while Moriarty had since received a knighthood and was now Sir James! I balked at the effrontery of it all.

I knew now Watson, that I must find you, and together perhaps, we could make something of this most strange and disastrous turn of events. I tried to locate you at the usual haunts, at St. Barts Hospital, your office on St. Anne's Street, even at your old regimental stomping grounds. No one had seen you for months. Some told me a sad story of how you had fallen on hard times, that you had taken the news of my death badly, that you had fallen to drink. I was shocked. Astounded, really. It was most unlike you, old boy, to overindulge in spirits at all. To allow yourself to become so wedded to drink as I was being told was quite incomprehensible to me. At first I did not believe it at all. However the rumours I heard in my travels told me of a once proud doctor of medicine who had descended deeply into the dubious comfort afforded by the bottle.

And so it necessitated a change of tack, and I began to seek you out in those more wretched establishments frequented by denizens of our grand city who look to drown the past, and their own place in it, with drink.

I tell you, dressed as I was as a hapless old salt of the seven seas, I was able to fit in quite well with those who frequented such establishments and find out many interesting tidbits as I tracked you down. The most disturbing of which is that the common folk believe Good Queen Victoria had been murdered and the crime covered up. The people hate King Eddy, and they are restless and fearful. Many believe he seeks to restore the monarchy to its full power, and that soon now he will disband Parliament and ask for the resignation and abolishment of the office of Prime Minister. That is surely incredible, and I put these rumours to the superstitions of the common folk and less educated classes. Yet they believe them firmly, I can tell you. A dark pall seems to have descended upon our city — a dark pall, I would wager, by the name of Moriatry.

But first things first. I had to find you, Watson, and in this most effective disguise it was but a day later that I was to stumble into the *Cock & Crow*, a shabby East End pub. There I saw a sight I thought I would never see in my life. There I saw a familiar figure seated at a lonely table, slumped down and obviously unconscious from too much drink.

I approached carefully, and nudged you awake.

You looked up annoyed, your eyes red with drink and barked, 'Move on! Move on! Can't you see I want to be left alone in my misery!'

My heart broke to see you like that, old friend, rank and dishevelled, bleary-eyed and forlorn. Nothing but a hopeless drunk. You'd have hardly fared worse had you sunk to the opium pipe.

I sat down opposite you and looked you over. You had not changed much in my absence and yet you had changed significantly, and for the worse. You looked terrible, but I hoped it was nothing a bath, shave, and good food would not cure.

'Barkeep! Barkeep!' I ordered, 'Bring us a pot of your strongest coffee!'

'Aye, mate, coming right up,' the barman replied.

Then your head rose off the tabletop and you made a valiant effort to focus your eyes across the small table to see who I was.

Of course I was in disguise and you did not recognize me.

'Be gone! Leave me alone!' you barked. Then your head dropped back to the tabletop barely conscious.

The barman brought over a pot of steaming coffee. I poured a large cup and set it down in front of you.

'Drink,' I ordered.

You looked up at me again, let out with a curse, moved to grasp the nearby whisky bottle on the table, which I promptly dashed to the floor in a dozen pieces.

'Hey! What the . . . ?'

'Drink the coffee, Watson!' I said firmly. 'I need you sober and keen of mind.'

Well that got your attention. Your head rose off your hands and you took a second look at the old salt in front of you. Your head swayed with the affliction of too much drink but you steadied your gaze long enough to see through my disguise.

'Holmes?' You whispered in a low and fearful gasp. 'Can it be?'

'Yes, good Watson, it is I, but keep my disguise in order, I do not want to be found out yet.' I said.

'But . . . but you are dead?' you stammered.

'Not quite yet,' I tried to reassure you.

'Then you must be some hallucination?'

'Watson, really!' I replied sharply.

Then your eyes grew wide as saucer plates, and a tiny smile broke through your cracked lips. Tears streamed from your eyes.

'Holmes.' You whispered, 'Holmes.'

'Sssshh!' I warned.

'Yes, I understand.'

I had found you, my good Watson, my anchor in the world!

* * *

After half a dozen cups of the barman's strong but brutal brew, your demeanour and state of mind slowly came back to that which I know and love.

'Holmes! I cannot believe it!'

'Keep it low, my friend. It is to both our advantages that certain people continue to believe me dead. Call me . . . Sigerson.'

You nodded, tried to clear your mind and finally asked, 'But you are alive. So tell me, what has happened?'

I smiled, 'That is what I hoped you could tell me?'

You were quiet for a long moment, thoughtful. Then said, 'Yes, much has transpired since you left. But how can this be? You are dead! What happened in Switzerland?'

'Obviously I am quite alive, Watson. Nevertheless, that is an adventure I will relate to you in its entirety some other time. Right now you have to answer me this one question.'

'Anything.'

'Watson, I have been gone long by some standards — but surely not long enough that such fantastic events should transpire in the world. In London.'

'I take it you have been to 221B?' you said sheepishly.

'Indeed, what is left of it.'

'So you saw . . . '

'I saw the results of a fire. I also know of the murder of Mycroft.'

'I am sorry.'

We were silent for a time.

'Now, Watson', I asked, 'tell me truly. What has been going on here while I have been gone?'

You steadied your hand as you took another reassuring drink of the hot coffee. 'It's terrible. The queen is dead, the new King, Eddy is a lascivious libertine. You should hear the rumours about him, if but half are true, he is a monster.'

I nodded.

Then you looked around, carefully,

whispering to me, 'Have a care. The king has agents everywhere. Secret police agents.'

'Really?' This was news. That certainly smacked of Moriarty.

Then you whispered fearfully, 'England, the world, we seem to be in the grip of some dread dilemma and I fear where it all may lead.'

'Moriarty is the source of this particular dilemma,' I said in a low tone. 'With my absence and supposed death no one could stand against him or his plans. With Mycroft murdered, our enemy was left to indulge his boldest and most devious devices. He apparently has done so quite well, and on a worldwide scale.'

'What do you want me to do . . . Sigerson?'

'Do you still have your revolver, Watson?'

'Of course,' you replied, perking up at the prospect of action.

'Where are you living now?' I asked.

'I have a small room at the Whistle and Thump, four blocks away.'

'Good, go to your room now and rest. I

will meet you there tomorrow,' I said, 'And Watson, stay sober.'

'You have no need to worry about me now, seeing you here and alive is the one true medicine for my sick and tortured spirit.'

'Good old Watson, together we shall work through this conundrum.'

⋆ ⋆ ⋆

Seeing you again, old friend, had done much to revive my own sagging spirits, but to see the state to which you had sunk with drink had not only saddened me, it had surprised me as well. It also got me to thinking. It really was most unlike you.

In fact, it seemed to me now there were many events, even given Moriarty's unrestricted activity, that did not add up. Mycroft dead? Assassinated? Once I got over the shock of that, the more I thought about it, the more it seemed quite impossible. Our rooms at 221B burned and boarded up? Well that was a shock, but it was always a real possibility. What was not a possibility was that I was apparently both alive *and* dead. Then there was the Queen's death, was it murder? Moriarty's knighthood, the turmoil in America and elsewhere. My body in Moriarty's coffin! All most incongruous events as far as the facts I knew in my world.

It just didn't add up. These things I have mentioned could never all have happened in the world I knew. Something was amiss, and I fear that you are a factor as well, Watson, one more piece of evidence for the thesis I have reluctantly come to put on the table as a probable explanation for these strange events. Until this moment I had been loath to seriously mention my thesis in this narrative. You see, I know you. I know there is no way that the man I know would become a hopeless drunk. Not in my world. Therefore, you are *not* the man I know. You may be Watson, but you are not *my* Watson. You are . . . *another* Watson. And therefore, with the evidence of my body in that grave, and Moriarty alive, I must be *another* Holmes!

Following this reasoning, I knew that

Moriarty was not *my* Moriarty either. I also knew I must exercise extreme caution now. I had much to think upon. This was certainly becoming quite the three-pipe problem.

When you and I met next morning at your room, you looked much improved and I explained most of this to you. I told you my theory. I added, 'I now believe that my falling through the mists at Reichenbach had somehow transferred me into a different world. Your world. A world that is almost exact to that which I know, but with jarring differences.'

Your response, at first, was entirely expected. 'It seems preposterous, Holmes, utterly, and incredibly unbelievable. I am sure it was your body I had buried.'

'*Not my body, but* another. *I tell you, somehow I have entered your world, which is separate from my own. If you do not believe it, Watson, at least believe that such a thing can be possible. For how do you explain that I am here before you?*'

You thought this over knowing I was serious about it. I could see that even if you did not entirely believe my fantastic tale, you *wanted* to believe it.

'Nevertheless, old friend, when you eliminate the impossible, whatever remains, however improbable, must be the truth.' I said. 'I put it to you, your world and my world being the same place, that is impossible. It cannot be. Therefore these worlds exist *separately*.'

'I do not know, Holmes. Truly, I have seen and heard many strange things in my service in the medical field and during my war service in Afghanistan and the Far East. This however, is simply incredible.'

'Yes it is, but mere incredibility does not negate the truth of the matter. Something strange happened at Reichenbach. Moriarty and I fought. In your world *and* mine. In mine, *he* fell and died. In yours, *I* fell and died. At the same time, in my world I fell into the mist but did not die, instead I was somehow transferred here, to your world. A parallel world, or an alternate one, Challenger would surely be able to explain it better than I. That has to be why when I exhumed the body of the Englishman who died at Reichenbach, it was not Moriarty as it *should* have been — as it *must* have been if I was in my own world. It was myself! I tell you I was quite shocked at the time, but I knew that it was a very significant fact. It was my body in the coffin! It should by all accounts and logic, have been Moriarty's! That was the key that set me upon this course and raised many strange questions. Events since have only forced me to consider this thesis more seriously.' I concluded.

'I hardly know what to say.'

'Then don't say anything, but think about it,' I continued. 'However fantastic, my thesis must be true. As improbable as it sounds, it is the only one that fits all the facts. The icing on the cake was seeing you, old man. Seeing to what depths you had fallen after my 'death' alerted me to one simple but incontrovertible fact. While you are surely my good friend, John H. Watson, you cannot be *the* John H. Watson I have known for so many years. Hence the corollary, that this world is *not* the world I have known for so many years either. Therefore I am the outsider here, lost, stranded in *your* world.'

'Holmes, but if what you say is true, then . . . '

'Yes, Sherlock Holmes did indeed die at the Reichenbach. It was his body I saw, it was his body you saw — and let me tell you, there can be no mistake — it was the corpse of Sherlock Holmes. *Your* Sherlock Holmes.'

There was a long silence.

You nodded final acceptance, and I noticed a deep sadness creep into your features once again. Finally you looked at me with determination and even managed a wan smile.

'You are a doppelganger of my own Watson, or I of your Holmes, if you prefer. It does not matter much now so long as we understand it and what it means. Buck up, all is not lost. Quite the contrary, in fact. For instance, I believe your descent into drink may have actually worked in our favor, for it certainly saved your life.'

'How so?' You asked.

'Simply put, Moriarty held back on his revenge against you for I am sure he reveled in your self-destruction. Such would fit his warped ego and sense of justice, and it saved you from his henchmen. So now, here we are, both alive, and none the worse for wear.'

'Well, Holmes. It is good to have you back, wherever you are from,' you said, managing a good-hearted smile.

'Good man, Watson. It appears the game is afoot once again. And the name of this particular game, is Moriarty. I accept the fact now that this is not my world and I do not belong here. More than anything else I want to find a way to get back to my own world. But first, I cannot in good conscience leave this world to its own devices with Moriarty unleashed without doing something to restrain or stop him. Are you with me?'

'You know I am, Holmes.'

'So now we must determine what Moriarty's game is. That is what we must ask ourselves, for only then can we thwart those plans and bring him to justice,' I said.

'More crime?' you suggested, rather lamely, I am afraid.

'Not merely crime. It's rather beyond that now, if you keep up with what is being written in the popular press. I study the papers every day. It is rather amazing. The worldwide turmoil, and worse on the horizon, indicates some worldwide controlling factor. That can only be Moriarty. I really must say that the Moriarty of your world, has far eclipsed the Moriarty of my own in his boldness and in his accomplishments.'

'Well, I certainly never expected you to compliment him, Holmes.'

'And why not? He has achieved much in a short time. I am afraid we have our work cut out for us.'

'It certainly sounds that way.' Then you gave me a determined look and said, 'I am ready to help you any way I can.'

'Bravo!' Then I added, 'But we must take care here. Moriarty and I seem linked in some way I cannot yet understand, but it has to do with how I came here. I must be sure that whatever I do to stop him will not interfere with my being able to get back to my own world.'

'I do not understand, Holmes.'

'Simple enough,' I replied. 'Moriarty and I are linked, simply killing him may stop his plans, but I am afraid it might strand me here forever. That will not do. I fear if I kill him, it must be in a very specific manner. Perhaps I must draw him out somehow, for one final encounter.'

'Then what shall we do?'

'First, I have a little errand for you to perform,' I said.

It was not soon thereafter that you were off to Scotland Yard, while I sat down and wrote a letter to a mysterious Far Eastern visitor whom the papers told me had lately arrived in London.

It was with dire alarm that I listened to the news upon your return from Scotland Yard two hours later. You looked bleak and were reticent to speak and I had to prompt you a bit impatiently.

'Well, come out with it! What of Lestrade and Gregson?' I said. We were seated in your small East End room. It was a pale replacement for our luxurious lodgings at 221B, but it would have to do. 'Did you see them and ask them to come here?'

Well, you were quite upset from what you had learned. I had a bad feeling about the entire business from the looks of you.

'Watson?' I prompted. 'Are you all right?'

'Holmes,' you replied, 'I never saw Lestrade, nor Gregson. They were not at the Yard. When I inquired, I was told they had both been sacked.'

'Sacked!' I blurted, the surprise even affected my normal level demeanour.

'Yes, the new administration, Holmes . . .'

'What *new* administration?' I began pacing the small room now, longing for my pipe, or even the cocaine needle.

'You see, I made certain enquiries, very discreet, never mentioning your name or mine. It is incomprehensible! His Majesty The King has appointed a new commissioner of Scotland Yard. At first I found out that the new man was a war hero, a retired Army officer, even a big game hunter, and I thought . . . '

'Yes, well, out with it now, Watson!'

' . . . but no, they told me his name was . . . Colonel Sebastian Moran.'

I had to sit down. 'Moran?' I whispered. 'There's Moriarty's hand in that for certain.'

'It gets worse. Moran has shaken up the entire Yard, he has sacked Lestrade, Gregson, and others that you have had good relations with over the years. I heard he is expanding the force of secret police agents and giving them special powers. I fear he has doomed the Yard.'

'Indeed, now for certain the wolf is guarding the hen house and I am fearful for the good people of our fair London.'

There was not much more to say. For a long moment we were quiet, thoughtful.

'What do you want me to do, Holmes?'

'I will seek out Lestrade and Gregson. Now that they are unemployed, they should be at their residences. I'll try Lestrade first.' I said. Then I handed you the envelope that contained the letter I had written but an hour before. 'You shall hand deliver this message to our distinguished foreign visitor. He is in Room 600 of the Grand Hotel, and I want you to await his response.'

You nodded and looked dubiously at

the envelope and the strange name written upon it, saying, '*Thubten Gyatso, Ocean of Wisdom?* What does it mean, Holmes?'

'Deliver it, Watson, then meet me back here this evening.'

⋆ ⋆ ⋆

Inspector Giles Lestrade had a small flat off Great Russell Street. I made my way there through the streets of London. I continued wearing my disguise; grey beard, stringy grey lock wig, a bulk suit that made me appear to have 50 pounds of additional weight. For all intents and purposes I was an old retired sailor who had seen better days. I walked with an unsteady gait. No one on the street approached me, or paid me even the least attention, just as I wanted it. Carefully I made my way from your tiny East End room to central London and the Great Russell Street environs.

Greater London seemed not to have changed at all since I had been gone, at least on the surface. However underneath all the fine buildings and statuary, the busy crowds and traffic of hansom cabs, and the bustle of big city life, I noticed with great trepidation those small and disturbing items that made up that dark pall I felt had enshrouded the city.

While there had not been any substantial change, changes were evident to me. There was a new meanness in the people and fear I could see in their eyes. I had never seen such before in the good people of London. To be sure, people went about their daily business as they always have, but more than ever, they did so without paying attention to anyone else around them. Like horses with blinders on, they did not talk to strangers, they did not ever look in another's eyes. And the police and constables — well, I could see that people feared them now as they had never done so before — and even more so the plainclothes detectives of the Yard. As you said Watson, these seemed to have been organized into some form of secret police.

I saw it all with my own eyes as I walked the streets of London. The police now take people off the streets at all hours for questioning if it is even suspected they have made some negative remark against the King. I hear tell some of them do not return. The Tower of London has been reopened and is being used for a special type of prisoner — so-called 'enemies of the Crown'. Another special edict that the King has so directed. I have been told the dungeons below the Tower are full with malefactors who have been imprisoned for political crimes against the Crown without charges filed or any trial. Something our Good Queen Victoria would never sanction in all her years as our sovereign. Our new King seems to be seeking an expansion of the powers of the monarchy. With Moriarty an advisor behind the throne, it appears he and King Eddy are beginning a programme that will strangle our nation. I fear where it will finally lead.

Another item I heard in my travels through the city today; there will be a rally in Hyde Park to seek a redress of the people's grievances with the monarchy. It seems this could be the beginning of much civil unrest in our city. I was determined to attend that rally later in the day and see for myself what the situation was in this other London I now found myself a part of.

Meanwhile, upon reaching Lestrade's rooms at Great Russell Street I was surprised to see through the front window that the former Scotland Yard inspector was already ensconced with a visitor. I smiled at my good fortune when I noticed his guest was none other than Inspector Tobias Gregson, also now formerly of The Yard. Here indeed, was an opportunity to score two birds with one stone, so to speak.

Once more I relied upon my disguise as the old sailor, Sigerson. I could not give away my identity yet, and neither of these men would scarcely believe my identity in any regard. To them, like this entire world I found myself in, Sherlock Holmes was dead. I would leave him dead for a while longer.

I had to keep reminding myself that indeed, I was not *their* Sherlock Holmes, but was from another world, a different one than this, and that while my sympathies ran with the problems I had observed here, my heart yearned to be back in my true home. For in fact, this world was becoming more and more of a nightmare to me.

But now, first things first. Lestrade and Gregson were about to have a visitor.

Lestrade answered the bell, the little man looked as ferret-like as ever, his small mustache and nose crinkling up with distaste as he saw me.

'I do not accept solicitations, my good man. Now be gone,' he said as he made to slam the door in my face.

My foot in the breach prevented that nicely, and I responded with a powerful growl, 'Lestrade, I bring word to you from an enemy of your enemy. Be you interested?'

'Here now! What?' Lestrade muttered, perplexed, but it was Gregson who, standing close behind, put his hand on his companion's shoulder saying, 'I think we should hear what this man has to say.'

Lestrade shrugged and moved away from the door. 'Very well.' Then to me he said, 'You may enter, old man, and explain yourself forthwith.'

I smiled and said calmly, 'I serve the enemy of your enemy. My master must remain anonymous until a time in the future when it is safe for him to reveal himself.'

'Sherlock Holmes is dead, old man,' Lestrade said boldly.

'That, my good inspectors has yet to be determined,' I growled forcefully. 'But that is not a question to be answered now. What is important now, is that we confront Moriarty and his organization. He must be defeated or England and the world are doomed!'

'Moriarty?' Lestrade said, 'but he is the King's man now.'

'And the man behind the King's oppression of the people, and your own problem, Lestrade,' I replied boldly.

Both men stood quiet for a long moment.

'Fine words, whoever you are, old man, but we have been sacked, the King has appointed Moriarty's henchman, Moran, Commissioner of Scotland Yard, and we no longer have any official capacity,'

Gregson offered gruffly.

'Nevertheless, there are ways,' I said plainly. 'What I and my master want to know is this. Are you interested?'

'Aye,' Lestrade barked. 'I tell you at this point I care not for reinstatement to my previous position so much as I would like to wreak revenge upon those who brought this atrocity upon me. Gregson and I were discussing this very matter before you showed up, but we were at a loss what to do.'

'I believe that I can remedy that situation, with a course of action,' I said with a smile.

Then I told Lestrade and Gregson what I had in mind and they promised to meet me later that evening.

* * *

On my way back to your East End room, Watson, I passed by Hyde Park. It was but a couple of blocks from our old lodgings at Baker Street and there I saw throngs of people listening to speakers from various political parties publicly airing their grievances against the Crown and King. Such has been a custom in London and the Park for generations and often times it was merely the venue of fools or the unstable. But not today. Today there were thousands of citizens present from all classes and social positions who had felt the cruel yoke of oppression from this new monarch over the last year. In a rare effort, members of the Liberal and Tory Parties had united to seek redress against the Crown. I walked over to the speaker's platform in order to hear some of the grievances and listened with intense interest to one firebrand after the other describe acts that flew in the face of our good English law. I could scarce believe what I was hearing, but then I must remember that this for all its symmetry and exactness, was not my England, not my world.

I was harshly reminded of that fact when companies of stout London Bobbies, whom I noticed now uncharacteristically carried firearms, had been brought in to break up the crowd.

'This is an unlawful assembly and you

are hereby ordered to disperse immediately by order of the King,' the Captain of Police demanded of the crowd.

Well, the speakers began to incite those assembled to taunt the police and soon the crowd was booing and telling them to leave. To my consternation, I noticed light cavalry that could only be from the Royal Household Guard forming up at the edge of the lake. This was not a positive development.

There was alarm and concern growing now in the faces of the crowd as well. The police captain demanded once more, 'You have been ordered to disperse immediately, or face the consequences.'

Well, this was a fine pickle I can tell you, but matters got far worse when some in the crowd went from booing the constables to throwing objects. What happened next can only go down in the history books as a day of bloody murder. For the Household Guard drew their sabers and moving upon the crowd suddenly burst into a wild charge with points down and out. The effect was dramatic and disastrous, and after ten minutes of chaos, I could see there were dozens killed and hundreds wounded.

The remnants of the crowd along with the various speakers had become a mob and its members were being herded forward and arrested. I was able to make my way to safety along the lake. Many others were not so lucky. God knows where those arrested were taken or what was done with them.

As I walked the streets of London on my way back to your room, I could not fathom the nightmare world this was. With Moriarty unchecked, it appeared that civilization itself might be doomed.

⋆ ⋆ ⋆

When I returned to your room you were there waiting for me.

'Holmes! My God! What has happened to you? You look like you have gone through the Battle of Waterloo!'

'Not Waterloo, Watson, The Battle of Hyde Park. I suspect you will read about the massacre at the hands of the King's troops in tomorrow's *Times*,' I said, as I began to clean myself and change my clothes. 'But tell me, my friend, did you see Thubten Gyatso and deliver my letter to him?'

'Yes, I did. He is a very old man and had to have the boy at his side read and translate your message to him.'

'Indeed, that is most interesting.' I could not help but raise my eyebrows in curiosity at that inconsistency.

'Holmes?'

'Never mind,' I replied. 'But tell me, what was his reply?'

'His reply was one word, 'Yes''

I sighed deeply, in truth I had hoped it would not be so, but knowing the facts as I knew them to be, I had to discover what part our faraway visitor played in this strange series of events.

'We must leave at once, for I believe he may be in danger. Thubten Gyatso may also be the one person in the world who can answer my questions and perhaps help me return to my own world. We must speak with him immediately.'

* * *

We had to walk a number of blocks before we could acquire a growler with a driver who would deliver us across town to The Grand Hotel. The hotel was an imposing pile, one of the tallest buildings in London with six floors. We took the new 'lift,' or as the Americans are calling it these days, the 'elevator,' to the top floor. That floor was actually taken up by an entire suite of rooms for the express use of His Holiness and his rather large retinue of monks and servants.

We were led by one monk, apparently acting as a major-domo, to wait in a small anteroom while our request for an audience with the Ocean of Wisdom, as he was reverently called, was being considered.

'Ocean of Wisdom, Holmes? Who is this strange man?'

'Not man, Watson, for he is but a boy of 16 years. His name was Thubten Gyatso in his mortal form, but he is better known as His Holiness the Dalai Lama of Tibet. He is the 13th in a line of Dalai Lamas said to be reincarnated from that first of the line back in the 15th Century.'

'But what of the old man I was introduced to?'

'That old man presented to you as His Holiness was but a stand-in. He was obviously assuming the role for purposes of protection, assuming the target for any assassination attempt to save his master's life.'

'I see. Rather mysterious, is it not?'

'To be sure. That 16 year-old boy has travelled thousands of miles here to London. That is an extremely unusual journey for one of his vaulted status and implies great danger in some manner or form. I believe he knows something about my situation here. I do not know how that can be, but I feel he may be able to help me.'

'How so, Holmes?'

'The Tibetan form of Buddhism is a powerful force for peace and love, as well as the spirit of harmony and justice in the world. They have a long history of spiritualism and knowledge in many esoteric matters, and can detect changes in the flow of worldly events,' I added.

'Well, what was in your note to him?

Did you ask him if he knows how you can get back to your own world?'

'No. When I read in the *Times* that His Holiness had come to London, I knew it could be no mere coincidence. After all, Moriarty and I are in London. This entire scenario of events has London as its nexus. So I asked him, was his reason for coming here because he had detected certain anomalies in the flow of worldly events? As you say, his answer to that question was 'Yes.' That is an admission I find very interesting. I also wrote that if that was his answer, then he should take precautions because his life might be in danger. That is why we are here this evening.'

'What can we do, Holmes?'

'Fear not, we have allies, and I have placed them surreptitiously to unmask any danger. But hello, here is the major-domo returned and he is indicating that we are to follow him for our audience with His Holiness.'

The central room of the hotel suite was large and set up as a richly appointed audience chamber in the Far Eastern style. Large and luxurious *thankya* tapestries hung from the walls bearing colorful images of Buddha. At the end of the room was an elegant but empty throne, and off to the side, standing in front of the large windows, stood a young man, shaven pate, dressed in a fine yellow *namsa* silk robe. Around him buzzed a dozen Tibetan monks, in orange saffron robes, bald of pate as was their master, discussing heated issues as we approached.

Thubten Gyatso saw us and motioned his followers to silence. They quickly formed up in two long rows on either side of The Presence, as he was also known, while we walked forward to meet him.

'Your Holiness, I am Sigerson, and this is my friend, Doctor John H. Watson, who delivered to you a note earlier today.' I said. We shook hands in the western form of greeting. I had read that His Holiness was very much interested in the modern world and Western customs.

His Holiness The Dalai Lama smiled graciously, he was but a boy, but there was a depth to his face, and most notably his eyes, that made you feel you were in the presence of a much older and wiser man. He was purported to be the reincarnation of the last Dalai Lama, in a line that stretched back to the first master, and I could almost believe it true.

He surprised us by speaking English with a decided British accent, 'Welcome, my friends. Yes, I speak English, Mr. Sigerson, a teacher at the monastery in my youth. I find myself fascinated by all things British and modern and so thought it best to learn the language of the modern world so as to experience it first-hand. But, to get to your question, the answer is, of course, 'Yes.' You are correct. You see, for centuries my people have observed visions of the future in the sacred Lake of Lhamo Lhatso at Chokhorgyal. It was on one such vision quest where I viewed all that has transpired and much that will transpire.' The Dalai Lama suddenly stopped speaking. He turned to his retainers, motioned to them, and quickly they began to file out of the chamber. It was not long before we found ourselves alone with the Dalai Lama.

Once we were seated facing each other at the other end of the room, Thubten Gyatso looked at me intently and said, 'You are one of the two men I saw in my vision. Your actions at the exact same time in both worlds caused a breach, a doorway to open between these worlds.'

Well, here seemed more verification of my theory, and even if I did not entirely believe, I knew this had to be the truth. Nevertheless I asked, 'How can that be?'

'Better you might ask, how can such a thing *not* be?' His Holiness replied answering my question with one of his own. He was silent for a moment before he continued, 'Two exact events, happening simultaneously in different worlds — but with opposite outcomes — may open a doorway between those two worlds. Then, it could be possible to fall through from one world to the other. Sigerson, as you call yourself here, you see far, so much farther than most. What does your reason tell you? What do your facts tell you?'

'That what you say may be true.' I replied quietly.

'*May* be true?' he prompted.

'*Must* be true,' I amended.

The Dalai Lama nodded his youthful head, smiling graciously, then added, 'The other I saw was your nemesis. I have seen all this and more in my visions, and fear for our world with your nemesis unchecked. My visit here, aside from a most selfish desire to see the modern world, was to see if I could alert those involved to correct this error.'

'What error?' I asked.

'In your world, Sigerson, you slew your nemesis. In my world, here, he slew you. That should never have happened. The combination of his living, with your death through that encounter, has caused turmoil in my world. Which has caused his evil to exert itself to its fullest. The equilibrium has shifted. You must set it level again.'

'I want to get back to my own world, Your Holiness, but if what you are saying is true, I cannot in good conscience let my enemy destroy your world. I know what he is capable of, I have seen the results of his handiwork. I agree with you,

I must do something to stop him,' I said.

'Then there is only one way to do that *and* for you to be able to return to your rightful world. You both are connected by the doorway. It is still open, waiting for you to return . . . '

'The Falls! That must be it!' you blurted, Watson, adding, 'Sorry, Holmes.'

'Correct, Doctor,' the Dalai Lama continued. 'Your friend must replay the passion of that original encounter once more, and this time you must be victorious. Seek the mist, that is your doorway.'

I looked into the weary eyes of Thubten Gyatso and there was an almost beatific smile on his face. Most incongruous, that young face, with such worldly old eyes.

'And now, Sigerson, tell me, what does that far vision of yours tell you about me?'

I was taken aback by his request, but I automatically replied, 'Ocean of Wisdom seems an appropriate name, and if your youth is any indication, I see great things in store for you and your people in the coming years. You will have a long reign.

You are wise. You are good. You understand evil.'

The stoic look on the Dalai Lama's face never changed as he stood up and said, 'The audience is over, may you be successful in your quest, Sigerson.'

As we got up to leave, His Holiness added, 'Doctor Watson, please stay one moment.'

Both men saw the look of surprise on my face. But I left you, Watson and exited the room to await you in the small anteroom we had been in earlier.

The monk who was acting as major-domo came in, said, 'Your friend will be returned to you presently.'

I thanked him and waited patiently. I was left wondering just what the Dalai Lama would need to speak to you about privately, out of my presence.

As I waited, I heard a ruckus in the outer hallway and suddenly Lestrade and Gregson entered the room and behind them were four brace of stout London Bobbies. They held none other than Colonel Sebastian Moran in irons, as Lestrade hefted a peculiar looking rifle in his hands. It was Moran's notorious airgun.

'Just as you said, he was across the street, aiming to get another shot off at the old man by the window.' Lestrade offered, 'The old man you said would be the target.'

'Is the old man all right?' I asked.

'Flesh wound, but it is enough to tie Moran and his gun to alleged murder,' Gregson offered with a smile.

'You cannot arrest me! I am the Commissioner of Scotland Yard!' Moran declared with substantial pomp.

'Not quite,' Gregson said triumphantly, 'We may not have official authority any longer but there are still laws against murder. This is a citizens' arrest, all quite legal. You have been arrested for the attempted murder of His Holiness The Dalai Lama of Tibet. The crime may not get you gaol at the assizes because of powerful friends, but your days as Commissioner of The Yard are quite over!'

'Take him away!' Lestrade ordered the constables and soon Moran was gone.

'Things will go badly for him, and better for Lestrade and me now,' Gregson said. 'Who knows, perhaps there will even be a reinstatement?'

* * *

Once Lestrade and Gregson had left it was not long before you returned to me, Watson, from your private audience with the Dalai Lama.

'Well? I must admit, I am intrigued. What did he have to say?' I asked, full of curiosity.

You seemed strangely reticent, but finally you simply smiled at me, putting your hand on my shoulder in a very touching brotherly fashion. 'Fear not, Holmes. His Holiness explained it all. He really does see almost as far as you do. We must find a way to make Moriarty return to the Reichenbach Falls.'

I nodded. 'But there is something you are not telling me.'

You ignored my question and so I did not press it. Instead my thoughts turned to the problem at hand.

I was thinking about that link between Moriarty and I. It made sense, and Thubten Gyatso's words seemed to validate the facts that I knew. However, getting Moriarty to the Reichenbach once again, and by himself without henchmen, could prove difficult, if not impossible. He was powerful now, he had a seat beside the King, and he was a brilliant criminal. My plan would be near impossible, but I would have to find a way to make it happen.

'Can it be done, Holmes?' you asked me, seemingly reading my thoughts.

'I do not know,' I replied. Then I told you of the events that had transpired in the last half-hour with Gregson and Lestrade arresting Moran.

'Moran?' you said, showing evident surprise.

'Yes, Moran with his airgun, the perfect, silent, assassination weapon,' I replied sharply.

'But why, Moran, Holmes? Does Moran know something?'

'No. Not Moran, Watson, Moriarty. He must suspect. I wonder what it could be?

Well, whatever the case, he will surely be alerted now that Moran has been taken out of the picture.'

'That seems a key move,' you ventured.

I looked at you, standing there, the Watson of another world and yet, so very much like my own true friend. 'Indeed, you are correct. Moran being taken out of the game is a key event. A move Moriarty will not be able to accept lightly. If I know my Moriarty, and I think I do, this event will disturb him no end. Perhaps we can play on that to good effect.'

'Well, Lestrade and Gregson made the pinch . . .'

'Moriarty knows Lestrade and Gregson would never be able to pull such a coup on their own. He will suspect something, see the hint of my hand in the action. He will send his agents to ask questions about the old sailor who calls himself Sigerson. That is good also. Perhaps we can nudge those suspicions a bit into fears he can not ignore.'

'How so, Holmes?'

'I feel the rumours of my demise have been greatly exaggerated and too long gone uncorrected,' I said with a smile. I had an idea, one that might not only solve the problems of this world, and my own, but yours as well. You had lost your honour and taken to drink for my death. Now you shall be vindicated.

'Watson,' I said, 'I shall cause Moriarty to suspect through certain circles that I may, in fact, be alive. It will draw him out. He could not resist finding the truth out for himself and settling this once and for all.'

'Bravo, Holmes! That will set them up in Piccadilly! But how do we do it?'

I was silent for a long moment. There was much to consider. I began to miss my pipe and the swirling clouds of helpful tobacco smoke that always offered surcease in such matters. I knew this had to be done just right. I could not overplay my hand by being too bold, nor be scant in my approach. Finally, I took out pen and paper and wrote three letters. The first two were almost identical. One each was addressed to Lestrade and Gregson at their residences. I told them that I was indeed alive, that it had been I who had directed them under disguise, as the old sailor, Sigerson. Then I explained your part, Watson, in my plan. I told them you had always been acting under my direct orders.

Next, the third and most important letter, addressed to Professor James Moriarty. The missive was short, simple and direct. It said, 'If you seek the truth, then seek that which is in the grave of Sherlock Holmes.' It was unsigned.

Then I gave you these three letters, and asked you to deliver the first two to Lestrade and Gregson. The third letter I instructed you to leave at a West End pub in the hands of the barman, Reynolds. I knew the message would not fail to get to its intended addressee and pique his interest. Then, over your objections, I solicited a promise from you that you would stay in London and await my return.

Immediately after, I took the boat train once more, to the Continent and Interlaken, alone.

* * *

The evening of the first day I arrived at the small village below the mighty falls and took a room at the local inn. There I set my plan in motion. I contacted good Hans, and that night we stole to the cemetery, opening a grave. We moved the body within to another location and closed the grave. It was empty now, save for one small item.

The next night, from a place of concealment using my spyglass, I kept constant vigil on the grave of Sherlock Holmes.

As I expected, I spied a tall, thin figure furtively approach the cemetery with an enclosed lantern after midnight. He was alone and he carried a shovel. I watched with interest as he dug the dirt away from the grave of an 'English Man, Died, May 1891.' The more he dug, the faster he dug. Once he hit the wood of the simple coffin, he stopped, brought his lantern closer, and deftly cleared away the remaining dirt. Finally he was able to open the casket lid, and after he did so, he stood motionless and silent as a statue. I could well imagine his consternation, for there was no body in the coffin now. It was certainly shocking, but then, that coffin was not entirely empty either. Slowly, the tall figure brought the lantern closer to the coffin and he peered down to look at something within. Suddenly he reached down and pulled out a small envelope. It was the one I had left there the evening before. It said simply, 'Moriarty' on the outside. On the inside was a small note, which he pulled out, carefully unfolded, and began to read. That too was short and simple. It read: 'Meet me at dawn, upon the heights overlooking the Reichenbach Falls.' It was signed with the initials, 'S.H..'

Moriarty crushed the note and envelope and in anger threw them into the empty coffin. He looked around him into the darkness, quickly extinguished his lantern, and suddenly let out a loud menacing yell of sheer animal rage. I have never heard anything quite like it in my life. It brought a grim smile to my face.

It was now far after midnight and I gathered my things together and began my trek up to the heights overlooking the

Reichenbach Falls, where I would await Moriarty, and our destiny.

* * *

Dawn at the Reichenbach is a beautiful sight, Watson, and I was surely sorry that you missed it this time. In my own world you had accompanied me to the falls, but then at the last minute had been called away upon some pretext by Moriarty, so that he and I would be alone. Now, no such subterfuge was necessary, for it would just be Moriarty and Holmes, as it was intended all along. Two primal forces engaged in the eternal struggle between good and evil.

I was out of disguise now, it was no longer necessary and I was dressed in my usual clothing, along with heavy hiking boots and jacket. It was quite chilly upon the Reichenbach, even with the sun having just come up.

I looked over at the falls below in order to discern the whereabouts of that strange mist I had encountered upon my first visit here, more than one year ago. To be sure, it was still there, a misty fog, that seemed to shimmer and shift as it moved to different locations along the falls edge. I began to surmise that if the strange mist encompassed properties of movement — or at least of being able to change location — then that might be the reason why in our original encounter in my own world, Moriarty had died in his fall, while I had fallen into the mist and been transported here. The mist had to be the doorway. It seemed quite possible and I found myself enjoying the evident logical solution to this most strangest of problems once and for all when I suddenly heard a footstep behind me.

It was Moriarty! He was instantly upon me, wrapping me tightly in his arms, pinning my own arms to my sides, as he quickly dragged me to the ledge.

'Now, Mr. Holmes, I know it can not be, but it is! You seem to plague me unto forever. Can I never be free of you? Well, I shall be free of you, Holmes. I killed you once, of that I was certain, and I'll kill you again, and this time you shall stay dead!'

'Moriarty!' I growled, shocked now by what I could see of him. For this Moriarty was not the old, bent over, bookish professor I knew from my world. This man appeared to be younger, and certainly much stronger. I was at a loss to understand why — but then why should it not be so? The Dalai Lama had told me that while this world was similar to my own, it was also different from my own world. Had I not seen so for myself? Suddenly I realized that this Moriarty had killed the Holmes of this world in their first encounter. He could easily do so to me as well. He was bigger, stronger than the Moriarty of my own world. I felt myself being inexorably dragged to the ledge. I heard the churning, roiling waters crashing below, felt the spray from the cliff, the sun blinded my eyes, as I was pulled closer to my doom.

'You'll not escape this time, Holmes! This time you go over the cliff and die!' Moriarty growled these words into my ear.

I tried to fight him off but he was stronger and held me tightly. I could not free my arms from where he had them pinned to my sides. I could not break his hold over me. It was then that I realized I *was* going to die. He was going to do it again! He was going to hurl me over the ledge into the falls to my death on the rocks below.

And then I felt a heavy blow, as if from some mighty collision and we were entirely spun around. Then, good Watson, I saw your face, and you fought with Moriarty.

'Holmes, I'm here, the Dalai Lama knew you would need my help!'

'I told you to stay in London!' I blurted as I tried to free my arms.

'Hah!' you laughed, pummelling Moriarty with blows from your fist as you tried to pull us apart.

Then I broke Moriarty's hold over me and I was free. Immediately I stepped in to shield you from his blows. You hit him again, and once again, causing him to move away backwards, where he seemed to hesitate, to lose his balance. Then as Moriarty slipped over the falls, I watched in horror as he suddenly grabbed your coat, and you followed him over the cliff.

'Watson!' I cried.

'Holmes, no need, I'm glad it ended this . . . ' and your voice diminished as you fell down to the rocks below.

I stood at the abyss, as you and Moriarty plunged down to the falls and instant death below.

It was over. I looked down and saw that Moriarty and you lay mangled upon the stones of the falls and were soon pulled under by the furious water of the river. Both of you were gone a moment later.

'Moriarty finally dead,' I whispered, shaking with sorrow, 'but at what price? My good Watson, dead! What am I to do now?'

And then the words of Thubten Gyatso came back to me, '*Seek the mist, that is your doorway*.'

I looked over and saw that the mist was about twenty yards away and I walked towards it as if in a dream. It was shimmering in a most unnatural manner, and I could well believe now that it might in fact be some form of transcendental, or supernatural, doorway between the worlds as the Dalai Lama had told me.

Moriarty in this world, and in my own world, was dead now. I had accomplished my mission. I wondered, had I been brought here for this very reason in the first place? It was a question I had no way of answering. Perhaps Thubten Gyatso knew more than he was saying? Perhaps he had told you, Watson, and that is why, stout fellow, you had disobeyed my order to stay behind in London? Yet, your disobedience had saved my life, and enabled me to accomplish that mission.

Now it was time for me to go home to my own world, where I belonged. The gate awaited me. Sadly, I was leaving behind a world where not only Moriarty and Holmes were dead, but so was your own other self. Yet now, more than ever, I yearned to be free of this nightmare world and be back home in my own London, with my own good Watson, at our own 221B, with Mycroft, Mrs. Hudson, and even dour-faced old Lestrade.

I made for the mist. Once it was stationary below me I looked carefully down upon it. I knew what I had to do. I could not live in this world. Not with my best friend dead — who had given his life to save my own. But what I was considering was incomprehensible as well. If I was wrong, I would be doing myself what Moriarty had just been unable to do. I could be killing myself, committing suicide.

I looked into the roiling mist below. I took a deep breath. The shimmering seemed to call to me. I thought of you, good friend, and home, and all the people I desired to see again, and I dove down into the roiling mist and into my destiny.

* * *

'Are you all right, Mister?' I heard a voice saying from above me.

I was coming back to consciousness slowly, breathing the chill mountain air, feeling the dirt and grass under my body, I felt my shoulders and body shaken. I opened my eyes and there I saw good Hans.

'Are you all right? A strange place to fall asleep, no?'

‘Hans?’ I asked.

‘Yes, that is my name. But how did you know it?’ he replied carefully.

‘You do not know me?’

‘No, Sir. Should I know you? I have never met you before this moment.’

I nodded, ‘No, of course not, you would not know me.’

* * *

On my way to London, I bought a copy of the *Times* and read it with a renewed sense of joy as I learned of the plans being set in motion for the Birthday Celebration for Good Queen Victoria. She was to be joined in the celebration by her son Edward, heir to the throne. I sighed with relief, the world I knew, the world I belonged in was here, and I was in my rightful place in it. I read with interest where a new American president had recently been elected, and there was nary a peep of military insurrection or succession; where the government of France was still in the usual turmoil but had not yet fallen; and where Germany and Russia were quiet. It appeared now that all was as it should be.

I also noticed a small item tucked away in the back pages about Eddy. He wasn't King here, just a minor royal. It said simply that Albert Christian Edward Victor, Duke of Clarence and Avondale, and grandson of Queen Victoria, had been hospitalized for a severe illness, previous to his sudden demise. Now it was rumored the notorious libertine had contracted syphilis and that it had been the disease that had slowly driven him mad. It appeared the disease had taken its ultimate toll on the young royal. Now, there was no way he would ever become king.

I closed the paper and put it away. The train was pulling into Victoria Station. I cannot express the joy I felt. I had been gone a long time. Now I was home again. Immediately I hired a hansom cab to take me to Baker Street and our rooms at 221B.

I had a story that no one — not even you, Watson — could ever chronicle, for who would believe it? But I give it to you anyway, my old friend. You may put the narrative among your other papers in that old lockbox of yours. Perhaps someday in the future the secrets of time and space will be well enough understood so that my tale may seem credible. It seems incredible to me already, even though I lived through it all so recently. And, as I said to you last week upon my return, it was good to see you after so long, my dear Watson. It was good to see you.

The American Adventure

Over the years many of my correspondents and followers of the cases of the Great Detective, Sherlock Holmes, have asked me to divulge the truth behind the retirement of my friend. At 57 years of age, Holmes was in full trim and vigour and still at the height of his powers; he was long cured of his difficulties with cocaine and had a multitude of successful cases behind him. Why then did he suddenly retire a few months later in 1912?

In an effort to quell the sometimes heated conjecture and various rumours which often fuel such rampant speculation, I have decided to write down these findings just as Sherlock Holmes told them to me. They contain answers that lie somewhere amongst those hidden secrets from his earliest days, from the very beginning of the Great Detective's career.

Part I: Baker Street

It was an early autumn evening in October of 1911. Sherlock Holmes and I, as usual, sat before the roaring fire in our Baker Street rooms in apparent relaxed composure. The rain outside had been dreadful all day; a pouring deluge interspersed with thunder and lightning, but inside all was warm and cozy. All was also very quiet. Consultations of late had been sparse and inconsequential since the successful conclusion of the Carfax Case. I had not seen Holmes since he had been called away up North and he had just now returned. With no cases pending, I was sure the present inaction had put my friend in an ill temper. He sat across from me immobile, silent, apparently wrapped in serious contemplative thought, but I sensed something deeper was disturbing him.

At times like these I knew better than to make small talk or interfere with his concentration. So I sat quietly, my eyes roving over the headlines in that morning's issue of the *Times*. There was nothing of interest until I spotted a notice that I thought might intrigue my friend, perhaps even shake him out of his dour funk and the gloom of that rainy evening.

'I say, Holmes, here's an interesting item. It's about the famous Doctor Bell,' I said quickly. 'You do remember him? The eminent surgeon and diagnostician?'

Holmes looked up at me rather sharply but uttered not one word. A dour mood certainly had a hold on him but I was determined to see if I could break that roadblock with a few words that might intrigue him and perhaps begin conversation between us.

I shook my head, 'It says here that he has passed away. A few days ago, on the fourth of this month, sadly his wife and son predeceased him many years before.'

Holmes took the news silently, motionless.

I shrugged. I did not know Doctor Bell, of course. I hardly moved about in those lofty circles, but many in my field knew *of* him and his pioneering practices. I even seem to recall Holmes mentioning him briefly in passing upon one or two occasions because of his brilliant methods of analysis and diagnosis, which I knew mirrored my companion's own talents in the far different realm of criminal investigation.

'I say, Holmes . . . ' I began absently, his continued silence causing me to look up at him when suddenly my eyes beheld the most incredible sight. While my companion sat silent and immobile — the epitome of some graven image of stoic unemotionalism — something seemed very wrong. I looked upon his face closely and in the flickering light noticed a gleaming line running down his cheek reflected in the scant illumination afforded by our fireplace. It was really quite extraordinary. Suddenly I realized what I saw upon his face were tears. Sherlock Holmes . . . was crying!

'My God, Holmes! What is it?' I stammered, surprise mixing with growing apprehension, for I had never seen my friend in such a state in all the years I had known him. I began to grow fearful with concern; his utter lack of response was unnerving.

I took a deep breath, then asked again, softly, 'Holmes?'

'John, he's gone from the world,'

Sherlock Holmes told me in a low voice that was sadness itself and did not sound like him at all. 'He was the greatest man that I have even known, and the best of all men.'

'Bell?' I asked curiously. 'You . . . knew him?'

Holmes nodded slowly.

'I had no idea, Holmes. I'm . . . very sorry,' I blurted, feeling his sadness.

'He's gone now,' Holmes repeated in a soft whisper. The deep sorrow in his voice and his grim visage seemed to fill our tiny sitting room with a pall of sadness that was a palpable thing. 'I must tell you that my recent trip up North was to Edinburgh. With all Joseph's family long since deceased, it was up to me to arrange the burial and a headstone with a proper inscription.'

I'm afraid I did not know what to say to assuage my companion's grief or how to react to this information, but then with a deep sigh he himself continued the conversation.

'I've never spoken of this to anyone, John,' Sherlock Holmes said. 'Doctor Bell was not only my mentor but a good and trusted friend. I shall mourn his passing as if he were my own brother.'

'I had no idea, Holmes . . . that the two of you . . . '

Holmes nodded with a wry smile, 'We go way back; it was many years ago, even before our own association. We not only knew each other, we worked together once.'

The storm outside was growing worse, the thunder and lightning a fit accompaniment to the pouring rainfall on that dark and moonless evening. I poured another glass of brandy, a liberal three fingers, as Holmes lit his pipe. His momentary lapse into emotion had apparently ended and now he looked up at me with a wry smile, seemingly his old self once again.

'Now, John, I will tell you a story I have never told anyone, about Dr. Bell and I, and our adventure,' he began in his usual strong voice. 'I owe all that I am and all that I have become to the good doctor and what happened when we went to America.'

'You have been to America?' I asked surprised.

'It was a long time ago. I was a young lad then of just 22 years, newly out of university, in fact. It was the autumn of 1876. I had done well in my studies but was at an impasse as to what career path to follow in life. I had a good grounding in the basic sciences of the day; however, I was young, emotional, and rather naive about life and love. It was my association with Dr. Bell and his methods that enlightened me. He told me I should become an investigator, what he termed a consulting detective.'

'I see,' I replied softly, but of course I did not see at all yet. 'So you and he worked on a case in America?'

'Not a case . . . it was more in the line of a little adventure we had. Actually, Dr. Bell originally wanted to enlist my brother, Mycroft. He had heard something of his talents, as he'd just entered government service and made a name for himself. Of course, Mycroft being Mycroft, while duly appreciative of the honour I'm sure — for even then Dr. Bell's methods had drawn attention in certain circles — was horrified at the very thought of travel. And such a long voyage! No, it would never do. Mycroft immediately declined the offer.'

'He declined!'

'Yes, and quite forcefully as I remember,' Holmes added with a thin smile now as he recalled memories from so long ago, 'then Mycroft recommended . . . me.'

Part II: Doctor Bell, 1876

'Well then, Mr. Holmes,' Doctor Joseph Bell said rather sternly, not at all trying to hide his disappointment, 'if not you, then who shall I engage in my mission to America?'

Mycroft Holmes pursed his lips, 'Why, I have just the man for you. He is young, eager, intelligent and ready to make a name for himself. None other than my younger brother, Sherlock. He's just completed his university studies and is exactly the man you need for such a venture.'

'Really?' Bell replied dubiously. 'So it seems if I am unable to have the Holmes I want, then I may have a lesser one as replacement?'

'I beg you not to think of it that way. I tell you in all honesty, you could not make a better choice,' Mycroft replied confidently.

To Bell that certainly remained to be seen.

* * *

The next day a meeting was held in the Visitor's Room of Mycroft's one centre of social activity, a venerable and odd establishment that went by the name of the Diogenes Club. It was an organization that boasted the most unclubable men in London. The younger Holmes had never been there before and the older Holmes seemed to spend an inordinate amount of time there these days — even more so than at his new flat in Pall Mall.

'He'll be here soon so please do try to make a good impression, Sherlock,' the older Holmes said in warning, 'at least for my sake. This is a great opportunity for you. I believe Dr. Bell is a man who will soon make substantial contributions to the Empire.'

'It's always the Empire with you, Mycroft,' Sherlock said testily. 'Personally I don't care, I'd rather pursue my studies. You know anything that takes me away from them I find to be an annoyance. And you say this fellow wants me to accompany him all the way to America of all places?'

'Yes, he is in need of a trusted assistant and partner in his travels. He will pay handsomely and the experience will do you good — even dare I say it — in your little hobby regarding the sensational press, perhaps even including . . . murder.'

Sherlock looked carefully at his brother at the mention of the word, now alert, 'Did you say 'murder'?'

'Perhaps, Sherlock, it is a most foul situation, but I shall speak no more of it now. I will instead allow Dr. Bell to tell you his own story in his own way.'

'Very well then,' Sherlock said quietly,

now at least willing to listen to what the man had to say.

It wasn't long before Dr. Joseph Bell was escorted into the Visitor's Room to meet with the Holmes brothers.

'Ah, Dr. Bell, so good to see you again,' Mycroft Holmes said welcoming his guest and taking his hand in a warm handshake.

Dr. Joseph Bell was a lean and tall man, sparse of build, there seemed not an excessive or wasteful bit of fat on him at all. He had the long and sensitive fingers of a musician. His steel grey eyes had a sharp focus to them; they could twinkle with mirth and good fellowship or become cold with stark shrewdness. Bell had an angular nose and a chin that matched. His voice was firm but tended to be high-pitched when excited. He was the type of man who walked into a room and commanded immediate attention by all, and he had that instantaneous effect upon the brothers now.

'Mr. Holmes,' Bell acknowledged Mycroft, though his eyes couldn't help but dart to the form of the younger Holmes who stood nearby, awkwardly waiting to be introduced. This younger Holmes he looked over carefully. He did not seem anything at all like his older namesake. This Sherlock Holmes was but a boy newly out of college, ruddy faced, tall, gangly, quite awkward and even shy. He stood by obviously uncomfortable, and it was just as obvious he had been roped into attending this meeting by his more forceful older brother.

And yet, Bell noticed there was definitely something special about the lad. The look of him, the sharpness and intensity of those eyes; they darted everywhere, examining, measuring, watching all. Bell could see this was a sharp lad with an inquiring mind and keen intelligence. A quiet lad, but he seemed to miss nothing. However, he was still barely a boy, much like all young men his age, undisciplined, mayhap too prone to the carelessness of youth.

Bell knew the type, and an almost infinitesimal grin escaped his lips, for he had been not unlike that young man himself at that age.

'And this is my brother, Sherlock,'

Mycroft said finally presenting the young man to the doctor for the first time. The two shook hands.

'It is good to meet you, Sherlock. I have heard interesting things about you from Mycroft,' Bell said pleasantly.

'And I about you, Dr. Bell,' the younger Holmes replied glaring at his brother.

Bell smiled at the bold audacious lad. 'And how is your research coming along with hemoglobin?'

Holmes looked back at Bell in surprise, 'How do you know about that?'

Bell smiled cryptically, 'Why, it is elementary.'

'Did you tell him, Mycroft?'

'Not one word,' the older brother replied defensively.

'Elementary?' Sherlock asked sharply. How so? 'Please explain?'

'Now, Sherlock . . . ' Mycroft interjected in stern warning.

'No, Mycroft, the doctor has made a statement of fact, and I would like to know from whence his facts originate.'

Mycroft sighed and shook his head in despair, fearing his young brother would mess up the entire interview.

Bell smiled indulgently, the youth was a bit arrogant, but he liked that in a young man, it showed determination and intelligence. 'Well, to begin with, I see two chemical burns on your index finger, a stain upon your thumb and one upon your pinky. These are of the type that could only be made by chemical reaction with human epidermis. I am after all a medical man, young Mr. Holmes, and do notice such things.'

Sherlock bristled at the word 'young'.

'Furthermore,' Bell continued with a smile, 'I can see you were in the laboratory this very morning working with blood samples. There is an insignificant but noticeable brown spotting to your right shirt sleeve and a fleck of spotting has remained on your neck, in spite of your valiant attempts to clean up before you came here for this meeting. I would venture the spotting is human blood. Am I not correct?'

Sherlock Holmes looked at the doctor with wide eyes. Annoyance mixed with wonder and surprise clouded his features.

Mycroft just laughed, his eyes twinkling with delight, 'Very well done, doctor, most enlightening!'

The younger Holmes looked at Bell carefully. In measured words he said, 'I have been endeavouring to discover a reagent that will determine hemoglobin from animal blood.'

'A lofty goal,' Bell said. 'Then your interest is of a medical nature?'

'Not precisely, though I do consider much in the medical sciences analogous to certain fields I find of interest,' Holmes stated.

'Well, now,' Mycroft interjected quickly, 'this is all very interesting I'm sure, but since I have pressing work to do I am afraid I must take my leave of you both now. Please excuse me, and do feel free to use the accommodations of the room to discuss your business.'

A moment later Mycoft Holmes was gone and the two men stood face to face alone in the room.

Dr. Bell cleared his throat preparatory to speaking but it was the lad who spoke first.

'I have been lead to believe that you require my services on some mission?'

'That is essentially correct,' Bell answered. 'The mission however, is quite unofficial.'

A thin, almost imperceptive smile came to Holmes lips, 'Murder is involved?'

Bell's eyes darted over Holmes' face, the young man showed no emotion, barely any apparent interest at all, but the doctor knew the lad was intrigued nonetheless.

'Perhaps,' he said. He sat down at one end of the large table, with a few chairs it was the only furniture in the room. He motioned for Holmes to sit opposite him. 'I believe it would be best if I began at the beginning.'

The young man sat down, relaxed, withdrew a pipe and began to stuff the bowl with tobacco. Then he set it afire and began puffing away patiently.

Bell smiled, the lad was a cool one, a bit awkward and shy, but he did hide it well. Very controlled in his own way but still so young.

'You see, Mr. Holmes . . . Sherlock,' Bell began slowly, 'I have a problem.

Someone very dear to me is in trouble in a foreign land and I am the only person she can count on for help.'

'Who is this person?'

'My sister, Diana. She is far away in America, in New York City to be exact,' Bell explained.

'And what is her problem?'

'You see,' Bell explained, 'I love my sister very much, she is older than I and I always looked up to her when we were children. She is only my half-sister you understand, from father's first wife, long since deceased. Diana has always been the black sheep of the family, bold, impulsive . . . somewhat troublesome. Father disowned her when she sought a career on the stage in London. I lost track of her when she left for America. Since the death of my dear wife, Edith, barely two years past, and with my young son Benjamin away at school, I find myself alone and craving those family ties we all cherish so much. Now I have heard this terrible news from Diana that she is in some trouble. She says her new husband is going to kill her. She needs my help, and I need your help.'

'And what do you require of me, Doctor?'

'Your assistance, your companionship in my journey to America,' he said softly. 'I need someone I can rely on, someone I can trust, but he must have a keen intellect and not averse to action if necessary. I credit myself a good shot as a sportsman. Can you use a revolver?'

'I am adequate with a pistol.'

Bell nodded slowly, 'And as for my choosing yourself for this deed, you must know my first choice was your brother, Mycroft.'

Holmes laughed mildly, 'Who quite strenuously refused you!'

'Quite so,' Bell admitted somewhat taken aback. 'However, he heartily recommended you, and now that I have met you in person, I admit I am not disappointed. I hope you will accompany me upon my mission to America. I will, of course, pay all expenses and your financial recompense will be more than adequate.'

Sherlock Holmes rubbed his chin

thoughtfully. 'A trip to America will take me away from my studies for weeks, maybe months . . . '

'Quite the contrary,' Bell responded forcefully, 'for if my method of deduction tells me anything about your area of interest, young Mr. Holmes, this situation will coincide perfectly with your chosen field of study.'

Holmes laughed sharply, 'And how, pray tell, Dr. Bell, do you know what that chosen field is, when I have not yet chosen it?'

Now Bell laughed, 'It is elementary, my dear Mr. Holmes.'

Holmes looked at him sharply, allowing his annoyance to show.

'Your future has chosen you, my boy,' Bell explained, 'and if I am correct — and I am most always correct — by the end of our journey you will know your path and see it as clear as I do.'

Holmes nodded, 'Alright then, Doctor, when do we start?'

Bell told him travel plans were all arranged. Tickets had already been purchased and they were to leave for

America the next day from Liverpool docks on one of the newest and fastest steamships of the White Star Line.

Part III: Aboard the *Oceanic*, 1876

'This really is quite an impressive vessel,' young Sherlock Holmes said as they strolled the deck of the mighty steamship.

The *Oceanic* was a beautiful three-masted ocean liner built exclusively for the White Star Line in 1870 and the first ship to carry transatlantic passengers in luxury and grace. She had promenade decks and even running water with bathtubs for passengers, this at a time when all other such vessels were nothing more than high-priced cattle cars. The £12 fare was reasonable for the day, and the 15 knots speed of the vessel ensured the transatlantic passage would be made quickly, in about seven days time.

'This is the forerunner of a quartet of such ocean liners, Sherlock,' Bell said appreciatively. 'I believe someday such ships will herald in an entirely new mode of transatlantic travel.'

They were strolling along the *Oceanic*'s luxurious promenade deck alternately watching the busy goings on among the other passengers and viewing the calm serenity of the Atlantic Ocean's gently rolling waves. The rough seas and rain of the previous two days had finally gone making this their first opportunity to enjoy the luxury of the ship's sunny and calm deck. It was a peaceful morning as they walked on, looking over their travelling companions.

Sherlock Holmes smiled, nudged Bell softly, 'Well there's an unsavoury character, if ever I have seen one.'

They passed a nefarious old fellow limping slowly along the ship's rail.

'Oh, I don't believe so, Sherlock,' Bell answered as his deep grey eyes glanced upon the subject of his young companion's attention.

'What do you mean?' Holmes asked.

'Well, the man's obviously a pensioned soldier,' Bell said, 'a sergeant by the looks of him. He has fought in India, no doubt wounded in the Mutiny and been sadly cast aside like too many of our heroic old veterans. He deserves our pity and favour, not scorn. Now he's seeking a new life in America and I for one applaud his industry.'

Holmes stopped and looked at the doctor squarely, 'So you know the fellow!'

'Why, I never saw him before this moment.'

'Upon your word?'

'Upon my word, Sherlock,' Bell replied seriously.

Holmes shook his head slowly, 'Then how do you explain all you have said about him? How can you know such things are correct by guessing?'

'I never guess!' Bell returned sharply obviously offended.

'I meant no insult,' Holmes quickly corrected. 'I just want to understand.'

'Well, it is all quite elementary,' Bell replied simply as they continued walking. The doctor's continued use of the word 'elementary' annoyed Holmes immensely.

Bell smiled at the young man, then added, 'Sherlock, I am as certain of the results garnered from my method as I am that you are standing here before me now. Facts and evidence tell me quite clearly that I am correct.'

'Well, the man seems rather a disreputable fellow, perhaps I should call the purser and have him removed? I'm sure he does not belong here in the first-class section,' Holmes said, but then thought better of his words when he noticed the disapproval on the older man's face.

'I wouldn't do that, Sherlock. He is on hard times and while I admit he presents a grim visage, he is harmless. But young man, you are seeing the fellow with your emotions and most superficially, I might add. To do so gives you a false picture of him. Rather, you must strip away emotions and feelings and observe only facts. Spot the details. Only by gathering facts and evidence can you ever deduce truth. Feelings will betray you every time, my young friend. Yet I see, like many your age, you wallow in your feelings and emotions.'

'The poets tell us to indulge our emotions and to trust our feelings,' Holmes countered.

‘‘The poets?’ Ah, yes,’ Bell said with a grin, ‘but the poets are wrong.’

‘How can you say that?’

‘Feelings will always betray you, mark my words,’ Bell said more forcefully. ‘I myself am regarded as a poet of some repute and surely appreciate the beauty and truth of poetry and human emotion. There is much there that is good, but there is much that is bad, Sherlock. Passion can cut both ways. A loving mother can bathe a child or drown that very same child in its bath water. I have seen too many examples of the latter. Wide open eyes are best these days, my friend.’

‘Well,’ Holmes said softly, ‘I’m afraid I do not agree.’

Bell laughed lightly but indulgently, ‘While you may enjoy the intoxicating scent of a rose, never fail to notice that a stinging bee may be lurking within.’

Holmes nodded his head thoughtfully, then asked eagerly, ‘Teach me your methods. Tell me about that soldier.’

Bell smiled, happy to take his role of teacher again, especially with such an eager young pupil. 'Well, Sherlock, it is all quite simple really. His clothing contains small articles of his past military uniform, I believe the 46th Regiment of Foot.'

'Ah, yes, I see the badge now on his belt,' Holmes said softly. 'I did not notice it before, it is such a trifling thing.'

'That's just it, Sherlock, you must always notice the little things.'

The young man nodded, looking at his older companion in a new light, 'Tell me more.'

'Well, if I am not mistaken, the history of that regiment includes the fact that it served during the Indian Mutiny in 1857. Where no doubt, our fellow received his wound. Note the limp in his right leg? The man appears almost 20 years past the retirement age so it is logical to assume he has been pensioned off since that time. Furthermore, he is apparently alone and without family. I believe he is on his way to America to make a fresh start in life like so many others in the New World. Why else would such a man be onboard in the first place?'

'How do you know he has no family?'

'Look at the fellow, his ragged clothing, his ill manner. No loving wife, dare I say it, no wife at all, would allow her husband to be seen in such condition. Do you see a wife, anywhere? No, this is a lone fellow, long ago cast off,' Bell said simply.

Holmes thought this over. 'What about the fact that you said he was a sergeant?'

Bell laughed, 'The right sleeve of his battered old jacket still contains the shadow of his stripes, long since removed.'

Holmes shook his head in disbelief. It was hard to accept all this at one time. He suddenly walked off and boldly went over to the limping man and engaged him in conversation for some moments. When Holmes returned his face was ashen, then flushed with excitement.

'So what do you think of my methods now?' Bell asked his young friend.

'You were correct in every instance!' Holmes said unable to keep the awe out of his voice.

'Well, good, it is rewarding to know that the diagnostic techniques I have developed for the medical profession may have broader application,' Bell said with a high-pitched laugh. 'Why don't you try it now, Sherlock?'

'I? Oh, I don't know, doctor. I neither know your diagnostic techniques nor have your patience for detail.'

'Then learn, young man! Observe,' Bell said sternly. 'Come on, what of that group seated in the deck chairs yonder?'

Sherlock Holmes shrugged, 'A mother and her children?'

Bell shook his head, 'You state the obvious, look deeper, Sherlock. Observe them, collect the facts in your mind, sift through the details!'

Holmes looked at the quartet more closely. 'It's interesting, a mother and her children, yet there is no husband or father with them? She's a woman of quality . . . '

'How so?' Bell prompted.

'By her dress, her clothing, and the clothing of the children.'

'And her behaviour?' Bell added.

'Yes, alright, so then where is the husband? Dead? Killed in military service?'

Bell grunted, 'Now you are guessing. Look closer.'

'She does dote upon the small boy,' Holmes said, watching more intently now. 'He seems ill. I believe he has consumption. My God . . . the boy is dying!'

'Yes, Sherlock, it is very sad. Of course, being a medical man I noticed such was the case right off. I see this sort of thing much too often. Now what of the husband?'

'A woman of quality would never travel alone without a proper male escort,' Holmes said softly. 'Therefore he must be here onboard.'

Bell smiled at his young protégé, 'Continue.'

'I don't know, there is not enough evidence to make a proper deduction about the husband,' Holmes stated carefully.

Bell's high-pitch laugh rang out happily, 'Precisely! Then what does one do when confronted with a lack of facts or evidence?'

Now Sherlock Holmes smiled, 'You seek them out.'

'My boy, you would have made an excellent medical man!' Bell said proudly.

Sherlock Holmes basked in the compliment.

As they walked on Bell added, 'Of course, it is not an exact science, Sherlock, but my methods do offer a place to start in making any diagnosis or investigation. So, admitting we do not have the facts, what do you extrapolate about the husband?'

Holmes was silent, thinking it through. They walked around the ship's bow quietly.

'A close family, loving wife and children, and the sick boy,' Holmes began softly, thoughtfully. 'I am not sure, but my best guess is . . . '

'Never guess, Sherlock. Make a diagnosis by extrapolating the facts that you have available.'

Holmes nodded, 'They had a fight, about the dying boy?'

'Perhaps, it would seem likely,' Bell stated. 'I see tension and tears in her face over her son, but did you notice how she kept looking back over her shoulder, as if waiting for someone. Yet not calmly waiting as if expecting her husband to join them, but anxious, yearning for him to join them. They had fought.'

Holmes looked at Bell carefully, then his eyes roved to the other passengers on the deck and then back to Bell with a sharp piercing gaze.

'Now what are you observing?' Bell asked him.

'You,' Holmes replied simply.

'Me?'

'Your methods to be more precise.'

'And what have you decided?' Bell asked.

'That they could prove most useful in my own work.'

Bell's shrewd eyes twinkled and he smiled with pride, 'Thank you, Sherlock.'

Holmes let out a deep breath and was about to answer when their attention was riveted by a shouting man, who they saw was a ship's officer.

'Doctor Bell!' It was the burly purser, Thorson, running down the wooden deck toward them. The man was out of breath and obviously frantic.

'Here, Mr. Thorson,' Bell shouted. 'What is it?'

‘You are needed at once!’ the man shouted, then lowering his voice he carefully added, ‘There’s been a terrible accident. A man is dead!’

‘Lead the way, my good man,’ Bell said and he rushed off with Holmes following quickly behind him.

When they reached the ship’s upper level, they were greeted in the passageway by a grim Captain Charles Morrow, ‘Nasty business, and on my own ship. I thank you for coming doctor.’

‘What is it?’ Bell asked.

‘Over there, inside,’ Morrow pointed into a nearby stateroom, the door was open and Bell entered.

‘His name is John Martin, a Yank returning to America. He has hung himself.’

Bell and Holmes walked into the room and carefully approached the body where it hung from an overhead light fixture. Neither man touched anything but each stood there observing the body intently as if transfixed. A belt had been hooked above to a chandelier and was wrapped around the man’s neck. He hung there slack, obviously dead, swaying gently with the rhythm of the ship.

'Jackson here, found the man,' Morrow explained, pointing to a steward who stood nervously behind him.

'Aye, and what a shocker it was, let me tell you,' Jackson piped up. 'I near lost my lunch at the site and ran straight away to the Captain with the news.'

'And you did proper, lad,' Morrow said. 'White Star does not want this type of thing getting out. A suicide aboard is bad for business.'

Captain Morrow motioned to the purser, 'Cut him down, please, Mr. Thorson.'

'No, wait!' Bell blurted suddenly, looking to Holmes for support. 'I think we should examine the body.'

Holmes nodded, 'Of course, the doctor is correct.'

Then Bell got to work looking over the corpse from various angles, then the rest of the room. He took out a large magnifying glass and observed the corpse even more closely, then the floor, and then he stood upon a chair and examined the belt around the dead man's neck. Holmes watched intently.

'Really, Dr. Bell!' Morrow expostulated, his temper growing short. 'This is all very unseemly.'

'A moment longer, I beg you, Captain,' Bell answered, but it came out more like an order and the Captain reluctantly nodded acceptance. Morrow watched as the doctor and his assistant observed the corpse as it hung there in front of them. When they were satisfied they had seen all there was to see, Bell looked at Holmes, 'You ready, Sherlock?'

Holmes nodded.

'Alright, Captain, you may cut him down now, but do so carefully and have your men place the body upon the table here. I want to examine it more closely.'

Captain Morrow gave the order and Thorson, with Jackson's help and that of another man, cut down John Martin and placed his body on the stateroom's short dining table.

Now Bell got to work, performing a minute medical examination upon the corpse and searching through the man's clothing as young Holmes watched intently.

'Sherlock, come here, look at this,' Bell said evidently excited.

As Holmes approached Bell took the young man's hand and placed it under the dead man's head, just above the back of the neck. The area was covered with Martin's long black hair.

'Notice anything?' Bell asked.

Holmes nodded, his eyes open wide in surprise, 'It's wet. It is very slight, very little, but it is wet. Blood?'

'Yes, but not enough to notice without close examination,' Bell replied.

Sherlock Holmes looked at the doctor and then back to the body on the table. Captain Morrow's face blazed and he quickly ordered his men from the room. When they were gone he closed the door and looked at Bell and his young assistant.

'What is the meaning of this?' he demanded.

Bell just grunted, examining Martin's eyes and face carefully, then he stated, 'This man was hit on the back of the head. It was such a powerful blow that it killed him instantly.'

'That's impossible!' Captain Morrow blurted. 'The man clearly hung himself, he is a suicide and shall be listed as such in the log.'

'The man was struck and died almost instantly,' Bell insisted. 'Then he was strung up to make it *look* like a suicide.'

'Mr. Martin was clearly murdered,' Sherlock Holmes added.

'That's outrageous!' Morrow barked now, aghast. 'It's a suicide I tell you. I cannot have any word of this getting out, it would mean terrible scandal.'

'What is more scandalous, Captain Morrow, is that you refuse to admit you have a murderer among your crew who needs to be brought to book for this crime before he kills again. Think about it.' Bell said, his high-pitched voice brimming with confidence.

Holmes looked over at his companion curiously, 'What makes you think the murderer is a crewman?'

Bell seemingly ignored the question, instead he said, 'If the captain will call in

Mr. Jackson then I shall demonstrate.'

Captain Morrow fumed; he was already measuring the implications of such a scandal to his career with White Star.

'Call the man!' Bell demanded.

The captain reluctantly walked to the door, opened it, and called for Jackson to come back into the room.

When Jackson entered the room Dr. Bell called him over, 'You say you found Mr. Martin hanging when you came here to perform your attendant duties?'

'Aye,' Jackson replied stiff-lipped.

'And you say that he was dead when you entered the room?' Bell asked the man again. He walked around him, his shrewd eyes examining the attendant's form and features minutely.

'Aye, I've plainly said as much,' Jackson said, growing nervous under Bell's shrewd gaze.

'Then where, may I ask, did you get *this!*' And as Bell uttered these words he thrust his hand into the man's jacket pocket and withdrew a gold watch.

'That's my watch!' Jackson shouted as he made a play to grab it back, but Bell was too fast for him and held it just out of reach.

Holmes remained silent but looked upon the watch as if it had suddenly been conjured up and appeared by magic.

Jackson blanched white shaking with fear now.

Bell handed the handsome and valuable timepiece to Captain Morrow. 'I believe if you examine this watch you will find that it belongs to the murdered man.'

Morrow looked over the watch, 'Why yes, it has Martin's name engraved right here on the back, it even says 'Presented to Mr. John Martin for twenty years valuable service.''

'No!' Jackson shouted.

'Mr. Thorson, place that man under arrest!' the Captain ordered and Jackson was soon held fast by the burly purser.

'How did you know?' Holmes asked the doctor.

'Once I determined the man had in fact been murdered, it was really quite easy for me to extrapolate a killer, based upon the facts,' Bell said with a wink to young Holmes.

They watched then as Purser Thorson took Steward Jackson into captivity and out into the hallway.

'I mean, *how* did you know?' Holmes persisted.

'It is all about access,' Bell explained. 'An American traveling alone, he knows no one aboard, well then, I tell you, his personal steward would have to be a prime suspect.'

'He promised me that watch as payment!' Jackson blurted from the doorway of the stateroom. 'He was into me for over a hundred quid.'

'Gambling?' Holmes asked.

'Precisely,' Bell replied. 'Well, Captain, you have your man and a murder has been solved.'

Captain Morrow nodded slowly, but he was none too happy, 'Murder aboard my ship, it's even worse than I thought, and by one of my very own crewmen. This will cause a terrible scandal when we reach home port in Liverpool.'

'Fear not, Captain Morrow,' Bell offered. 'A killer has been brought to book and justice was done. No one can ask better of the White Star Line than that.'

Morrow left the room pondering those thoughts dubiously.

'Well, doctor,' Holmes asked when the two were alone, 'answer me this one question then. How did you know about the watch?'

'It was a trifling thing, really,' Bell answered. 'When we looked over the body I could not find the man's watch, though a fob was clearly present. I thought that quite odd. I looked around the room, even on the floor, but could not find it. Nor could I find any watch in his clothing. So I knew it was missing because someone must have taken it. It just remained for me to find out whom. Steward Jackson was the logical suspect and the bulge in the jacket pocket of his uniform told me he was our man.'

'I suppose you would say it was all quite elementary, doctor?' Holmes said with a slight grin.

'Why, yes, I would, Sherlock.'

Holmes smiled, 'You would have made an outstanding detective.'

'No,' Bell replied softly, 'while medicine is not unlike detective work, I prefer to solve problems when the victim is still alive. You, however, seem to have a keen knack for it and I believe you should pursue that path.'

Part IV: America, 1876

'New York City, Sherlock! Look at it!' Bell stammered excitedly as they debarked the ship at a West Side pier. 'America!'

It was the American Centennial year, but 1876 was hardly a happy time in the young nation as most celebrations were overshadowed by the grim Custer Massacre in the West of but three months earlier. The tragic event had occurred upon the very day of the nation's birth. The daily newspapers were filled with news of the Army's hunt for the wild Indians responsible, even as this eastern city continued as it always had, with business and commerce abounding. With over one million inhabitants, New York City was as large and cosmopolitan as

London. And could be just as dangerous.

'Well, here we are and soon you shall meet my sister, Diana. You will like her, Sherlock. She's unusually intelligent and quite engaging,' Bell said full of pride.

'Where will we find her?' Holmes asked.

'On the stage, where else?' Bell answered. 'Quick now, we'll hire a cab and make our way to the Criterion. It is a music hall and the only address I have for her.'

Holmes did not reply but the look on his face showed a hint of his revulsion that Bell's sister should be involved in such an establishment.

'Don't be too harsh to judge, young man,' Bell added as they entered a cab and he gave the driver their destination. 'My sister has had to make her way alone in a hard and cruel world. I am sure she has had to cut some corners on what we would consider proper modes of behavior for a young gentlelady but her virtue is unimpeachable.'

'Of course,' Holmes replied, he had no wish to wound the doctor's pride, nor the glossy image he had of his sister.

On the way over young Holmes asked Bell just what they would do here.

'I am not entirely sure myself, Sherlock,' Bell replied thoughtfully. 'I only received the one telegram from Diana. The cryptic message begged me to come at once, that she was in mortal danger from her husband. I was not even aware that she had married, our relations had been non-existent since she had left for America many years ago. However, I know Diana, and she would not send such a missive lightly. I have not heard from her since that one message.'

Sherlock Holmes sat back in his seat, silent and in deep thought. The cab continued noisily over the cobblestone streets.

'I know what you're thinking, Sherlock,' Bell added softly. 'Why would I drop everything and traipse all the way across the Atlantic on such flimsy information? Well, I know Diana, if she says she needs my help in a matter of life and death I do not take such a request lightly.'

'And myself?' Holmes asked.

'I knew it would be best if I travelled with a worthy companion at my side, and one who could watch my back if things proved dangerous.'

'I am not a bodyguard,' Holmes said.

Bell nodded with a smile, 'Of course not, I just thought it prudent to travel with someone I can trust.'

Holmes nodded, satisfied.

Soon after the cab pulled up at their destination and they found themselves on the sidewalk of a wide and aptly named thoroughfare called Broadway, along which they proceeded toward a huge building that proclaimed itself with large garish letters as the Criterion Theatre.

Holmes was amazed by the structure, and even Bell found himself mildly surprised by the grandness of the building. The comely brick edifice stood boldly upon an entire block and seemed the centre for all sorts of activity, savoury and unsavoury.

Bell walked towards the front of the building, 'I'll be just a minute,' he said as he went inside. He came out a moment later with a wide smile upon his face. 'We're in luck, she's here, in her dressing room.'

The two men were led back stage by one of the ushers. There was no show scheduled for that evening, but there were many people in attendance and dressed in costumes for rehearsals, as well as what appeared to be the usual hangers on. It was a lively place, containing many beautiful young women and well-dressed young men seeking their favour.

'This is her,' the usher said, leading the two men into the back of the theatre and pointing to a red door with a gold star upon it high up in the centre. 'She gets a lot of admirers, so don't you be gettin' yer hopes up.'

A dark grimace overcame Bell's face at this not so veiled insult to his sister's propriety and morals. Holmes gave the usher two bits and quickly sent him on his way.

'Rude fellow,' Bell muttered, hoping not all Yankees would prove so crude, however his attitude immediately brightened at the prospect of finally seeing his sister after so many years. He gently knocked on Diana's door.

There was no answer.

He knocked again harder.

'Go away!' a strong feminine voice shouted from inside.

'Diana! Diana it is I, your brother, Joseph. I've come all the way from England as you requested,' Bell said as he opened the door and walked inside.

Diana Strickland looked at the two men who had so brazenly entered her dressing room. At first her look of anger turned to rage but it quickly softened when she realized just who one of the men was.

'Joseph?' she blurted astonished, running over to her brother. 'Is it truly you?'

'Yes, Diana,' Bell answered softly as the two embraced with a fondness that gave Holmes a brief twinge of jealously. For Diana Strickland was a wondrous woman of exquisite beauty and in the full prime of life. Holmes was breathlessly taken aback by her appearance and when her eyes shone upon him briefly, he seemed to feel himself melt before her gaze. He flushed as she smiled at him, then she gave her full attention back to her brother.

Sherlock Holmes took a deep breath as he watched this wonderful woman. He had never seen such a vivacious creature before, she shone with absolute radiance and sensual energy.

'Oh, Joseph,' she cried to her brother. 'Is it really you? After so long.'

'Yes, Diana, we came as soon as we could,' Bell added, holding his sister in his arms.

Finally she looked more closely at her brother's companion and smiled warmly, 'And who is this handsome young gentleman?'

'I am Sherlock Holmes.'

'Sherlock has been an invaluable assistant and travelling companion, Diana,' Bell explained. 'We had the most amazing journey which I'll tell you all about later, but right now we want to hear about your troubles and what we can do to help.'

Diana shook her head in evident despair, taking a moment to collect her thoughts. 'Oh, Joseph, I should never have contacted you. I'm afraid I've become embroiled in a disastrous situation that can only end badly.'

'You can speak freely in front of Sherlock,' Bell prompted. 'I trust him implicitly.'

Holmes looked at Bell in pleasant surprise.

'I don't quite know how to tell you,' Diana began. 'I know you and Mr. Holmes will think terribly of me for this and that perhaps I deserve all that an unkind fate has thrust upon me.'

'Let us be the judge of that,' Bell said softly.

'Why not begin at the beginning, Mrs. Strickland,' Holmes offered.

Joseph Bell's sister smiled, nodded, 'Of course, that would be best, Mr. Holmes. You just now called me Mrs. Strickland and that is where all my problems originate. For I tell you now, a dark shadow came over my life when first I met that man.'

'That man?' Holmes asked. 'Your husband?'

'Yes, my husband, Rupert Strickland.

You see, he is very wealthy, from a quality family, and they all hate me with a passion. While Rupert adores me, soon after our marriage he changed; he suddenly demanded that I quit the stage. We fought furiously over it and it has been a bone of contention between us ever since.'

'Well,' Holmes offered, 'you can not blame the fellow for that. He merely wishes the woman who shares his name to be a proper wife.'

'But, Mr. Holmes,' Diana said sternly, 'Rupert knew all about my stage work and my being an actress here at the Criterion. He heartily approved of my career and was my biggest supporter. He never missed a show and one of the reasons I accepted his proposal of marriage was because he promised to allow me to continue my profession as a stage actress.'

'But really, Diana!' Bell protested. 'You can not be serious. You are a married woman now and should follow your husband's wishes. You must be aware of the unsavoury aspects of your profession?

Why these 'women of the stage' are often nothing more than common . . . prostitutes.'

'Is that what you think of me, Joseph?'

'Of course not!' Bell blushed, the entire conversation was making him quite uncomfortable.

Holmes cleared his throat, 'I believe what your brother means is that you have to admit your profession has a certain unsavory aspect to it in the mind of the public — who do not know any better.'

Diana's anger softened, 'Yes, Mr. Holmes, there are those unsavoury people, but not all of us are like that, I can assure you.'

'Of course not,' Holmes said with a smile.

'Well then,' Bell continued, 'what is this problem? Your telegram was most vague and lacked details.'

'My telegram? You received only the one?'

Bell nodded.

'Joseph, I sent you three telegrams and five, no six, letters over the course of many weeks outlining the entire situation,' Diana said, a dark cloud covering her face. 'I was not aware his money and influence extended to the telegraph office and the U.S. Mail.'

Bell and Holmes waited.

'Well then,' she said, 'this is a pretty pickle I find myself in.'

'Then tell us everything now,' Holmes said. 'Hold back nothing.'

Diana nodded. 'My life was never an easy one back home, Joseph will attest to that. I was ostracized and disowned by our father for my profession and after Mama died I decided to come to America to make a new start. Here in New York I found what I had been looking for, a small but vigorous theatre culture that allowed me to sing and act in various stage shows. Many of them were quite raucous, and I admit there is pressure put on many of the girls to entertain important men, but I never succumbed. Until I met Rupert. He is young and handsome and it did not hurt that he is wealthy. And best of all he was never bothered by my stage work — until recently. I suspect that is all due to pressure from his family. They've always been against us, always trying to tear him away from me. They hate me and threaten to disown him because of me.'

'Well, what do you want us to do about this, Mrs. Strickland? We're hardly experts on marital relations . . . ' Holmes said.

'Perhaps if I talk to this Rupert?' Bell offered.

'It has gone far beyond that now, dear brother,' Diana said sadly. 'You see, divorce is not an option for such a family and now I fear . . . I *know* Rupert is trying to kill me.'

There was complete silence in the room. Holmes and Bell looked at each other and then back at Diana.

'That is a serious accusation, Mrs. Strickland,' Holmes said.

'Diana, how do you know that?' Bell asked.

'Events have moved quickly, gentlemen. Rupert has already been arrested and was released on bail. I assume he is now living at the family estate in Southampton, or at his hotel suite.'

'Arrested?' Bell asked.

'Yes, a month ago he paid two men

who came here to the theatre. They appeared at the stage door with flowers as do many admirers of the ladies who work here. They asked to see me and after bribing one of the stagehands to gain admittance, burst into my dressing room and tried to strangle me. If it weren't for the Director, and Burt, a stagehand, they would have killed me. As it was I escaped their attack and the men here caught the two assailants and held them for the police. I heard later the two men confessed after interrogation at the local precinct, admitting they had been hired by my husband to murder me.'

Holmes and Bell took in this information carefully.

Bell was angered, 'The beast!' he muttered.

Sherlock Holmes was less outwardly upset but inside his emotions were a bubbling cauldron. How could anyone seek the death of such a fine woman?

'Where do things stand now?' Bell asked finally.

'Of course Rupert denied it all, and his family came to his aid. They tried to buy me off with a rather paltry sum if I would drop all charges,' Diana said, looking from her brother to Holmes. 'You see, we are still married. The laws in this state while quite liberal still do not allow a woman to have much more rights than mere chattel. Barely a dozen years ago they fought a bloody war in this country to end slavery but I'm afraid women were never considered. And married women can be most tightly bound by law and custom. I cannot testify against my husband, I cannot divorce him. I had no choice but to drop the charges and hope he would just leave me alone.'

Sherlock Holmes shook his head at the injustice.

'This is very bad,' Bell growled.

'But that's not the worst of it, I'm afraid, dear brother,' Diana said softly. 'You see, I met Rupert barely two weeks past when he came to my room at Mrs. Shay's boarding house. She runs a clean house for proper young ladies and I had taken a room there after I was forced to leave him, fearing for my life. He demanded I come home with him and be an obedient wife. I refused. He vowed then that if I did not come back to him he would rather see me dead. I'm afraid I have no one to turn to, no one to help me. The police view the problem as a private affair between a husband and his wife. A family matter they are loath to get involved in, until as they say, an actual crime has been committed.'

'But what of the two assassins your husband sent against you?' Holmes asked.

Diana smiled, 'I knew you would focus upon them, Sherlock. May I call you Sherlock? The two men recanted their confession. Their new story is that I provoked them with salacious behaviour for a sexual liaison. I cannot imagine what gave them such an idea. They accused me of stealing from them, that they were merely trying to get the money back. It would have been a terrible scandal for the theatre so I was forced to drop all charges, if they dropped their charges. Then they were released by the police and that is where matters now stand.'

'That is a ghastly injustice!' Holmes said.

'And now you know, Joseph, Sherlock.

My life is in danger from my own husband and there is not one thing I can do to stop him. Until there is an actual crime committed with an actual corpse — *mine* — the police will hear nothing of it. I do not want to wait until that fatal moment to be proven right.'

There wasn't much to say after that. Bell and Holmes escorted Diana back to her room at Mrs. Shay's and then proceeded to their rooms at the Union Square Hotel.

Once in his room Bell asked his young companion, 'Well, Sherlock? What do you think? What can we do to help her?'

Holmes looked up, 'I'm not quite sure.'

'Well, I for one am going to visit this husband of hers first off on the morrow,' Bell stated. 'Diana gave me the address of his hotel.'

Holmes nodded, 'And what do you think about all that she has told us?'

'It's ghastly, Sherlock, ghastly that my own sweet sister should fall into the hands of such a monster,' Bell said, the anger stoking up in his face again. 'I take it you noticed the old bruises on her cheek and shoulder?'

Holmes nodded, 'I thought it prudent not to mention them, since she did not.'

'Yes, I thought the same though it galled me mightily,' Bell said in anger. 'I noticed more as we embraced, I could feel what seemed to be welts upon her back. I tell you, Sherlock, my lovely sister has been ill-used by this brute and he shall be made to pay.'

'Easy, Doctor,' Holmes cautioned, 'we should talk to her husband first. We need to get his side of the story and I would like to see just what type of man he is.'

'I know full well the type of man that he is, Sherlock,' Bell stammered in anger now.

Holmes only smoked his pipe and thought his own thoughts about the lovely Diana Strickland. There was still much left of the early evening so Holmes and Bell dressed and took Diana out to dinner. It was a wonderful evening with good food and fellowship as Bell's sister charmed the two men. Young Mr. Holmes discovered he was becoming quite enchanted with her beauty and personality.

* * *

The next morning Bell and Holmes took a hansom cab to Manhattan's very exclusive Fifth Avenue Hotel to talk to Rupert Strickland. They discovered they were in luck when the concierge told them that Mr. Strickland was indeed in his rooms. After a bellboy was sent up, the men were told that Strickland would see them. He occupied a suite of rooms on the fifth floor.

Bell and Holmes were escorted by the bellboy to a new contrivance that had just come into vogue then in New York, the Otis steam-driven elevator. This marvel of progress was described to them as a perpendicular railway that intersected each story of the building.

'Step in, gentleman, it's all the rage!' the boy said guiding them into the wooden boxcar.

'Amazing contraption!' Bell exclaimed, examining the strange device as the door closed and he and Holmes rode up inside it to the fifth floor.

'I have heard that the first of these

devices is presently in use elsewhere in this city, in the Western Union Telegraph Building. That elevator is said to rise the entire nine stories to the top floor of the building,' Holmes offered.

'Well then, we must make a note to ride in that one before our trip here is complete, Sherlock,' Bell said, then growing more serious, 'but for now we have work to do.'

* * *

They discovered Rupert Strickland to be a tall, thin young man with dark hair and a pencil-thin mustache. He wore a morning coat, smoked a cheroot and affected jaunty airs. A black retainer led the two visitors into his presence.

'Bell, Holmes,' he said. 'Good to meet you. You've come a long way I gather. All the way from London.'

'Edinburgh,' Bell corrected. The two men shook hands but the feeling was strained and tense.

'So you are here now, but for what reason?' the American asked boldly.

'What reason?' Bell blurted, hardly believing the cheekiness of the rascal, 'to protect my fair sister from the likes of you!'

Strickland actually laughed, 'Now that's a good one, sir. A rare one indeed! And who shall protect me from the likes of her?'

The remark caught Holmes and Bell off guard, but for quite different reasons.

While Bell fumed from what he saw as incredible effrontery, Holmes rebounded quickly and asked, 'It seems to me that you have quite a different story to tell from what we may have heard from your wife?'

'I'll say,' Strickland offered with bluff American frankness. 'I tell you that in all truth, you can't trust one word that woman says. She's beautiful as sin, but a witch of a woman, bad through and through.'

'I'll not stand here and have you insult my sister,' Bell stammered, evidently trying with all his might to hold himself in check. 'I've come here to speak to you as one gentleman to another, so that you will leave my sister in peace and refrain from harming her.'

'*I* refrain from harming *her*?' Strickland laughed in mock surprise. 'That is a good one.'

Bell was momentarily tongue-tied and flummoxed; he tried not to allow his rage to get the better of him from the absolute boldness of the villain. While not a violent man, Bell was surprised how much he wanted to pummel the fellow. At that moment he felt Holmes' restraining hand on his shoulder and the feeling passed.

Before Bell could say another word, Holmes quickly stepped in, 'Mr. Strickland, did you hire two men to kill your wife?'

'So you heard about that,' he answered softly. 'No, of course not. I did not try to have Diana killed.'

'So you deny it!' Bell demanded.

'Most emphatically, Doctor Bell!'

Holmes added, 'We can find those two men and question them . . . '

'If you can find them,' Strickland stated with a smirk.

' 'If?' I think you had best come clean with us,' Bell said sternly.

'What I mean,' Strickland explained, 'is that you will not find the men because Diana has surely sent them away. They're probably back in Five Points now. You see, they were her own men. I fear that my family was correct about my choice of a wife, much to my chagrin. Diana is a money-mongering adventuress. She has set her hooks into me to gain my inheritance and she very nearly succeeded. I fear that is the only reason she pursued and married me.'

'She pursued you!' Bell said outraged now.

'I see,' Holmes added with a smile. 'So then you have no interest in her?'

Strickland smiled, 'Yes, of course I did, at the time. I admit it. She is a beautiful woman and she can be most charming when there is something for her to gain by such behavior. We are still married but live separately.'

'Yes, we know. She had to leave you, to get away from your schemes,' Bell said.

Strickland shook his head, 'Doctor, I am afraid it was *I* who left *her*.'

Bell stared at him blankly, sudden

indignation growing rapidly in his features.

Holmes spoke up quickly, 'And what of her career on the stage?'

'It's true enough, she was to end all that after we were married,' Strickland offered. 'I thought she had done so, she had promised me as much, but she had made certain contacts through that world and she did not want to lose them. I fear they influence her overly much.'

Holmes shook his head.

Bell looked from one man to the other, then back to his sister's husband. It seemed the man was playing him for a fool.

'I do not believe you! Not at all, sir!' Bell said in his excited high-pitched voice. 'You are a dirty liar!'

Strickland's eyes blazed red at the insult. Suddenly his clenched fist struck out at Bell's face — but just as suddenly it was caught in mid flight and held in the firm grip of Sherlock Holmes' hand.

'Your violence is not necessary with us,' Holmes said forcefully holding the man at bay.

When Strickland showed he was no longer a threat, Holmes released his hand.

'I really wasn't going to strike him,' Strickland offered lamely to Holmes.

'Blah!' Bell huffed allowing his anger and exasperation full vent now. 'Just like you wouldn't harm my sister!'

This was getting them nowhere. Not only did the man admit nothing; he seemed the most natural liar ever placed on God's green Earth. That his sweet sister was married to a man of such violent tendencies made Bell grow more fearful than ever for Diana's safety.

They were at an impasse and soon Bell and Holmes took their leave. The two men rode in the elevator down to the hotel lobby, each deep in his own thoughts. Holmes could see the anger in Bell's face, but also a growing concern for his sister as well.

'You look troubled, doctor,' Holmes said softly.

'Of course I am troubled,' Bell replied in a low voice, 'the man's a devious and cunning devil and dangerous as a rabid dog. I fear more than ever for Diana's safety. She was right to have us come here, Sherlock, she's married to a monster.'

Sherlock Holmes kept his thoughts to himself.

'And Sherlock, my boy, I want to thank you for what you did back there. I never even saw it coming. You have keen instincts. I am sure you share them with the very best of police detectives.'

Holmes nodded, but Strickland's violence had him too worried to appreciate the doctor's compliment.

They exited the elevator and the hotel to hail a cab to take them back to their rooms. On the way Bell made the cabby make a stop at the Criterion.

'I think we will have a talk with some of the people at that playhouse, see what we can dig up about Strickland,' Bell said.

'That is a sound idea,' Holmes said. 'If you don't mind, I would like to speak first with your sister. There are a couple of questions she might help me with.'

* * *

Once the two men arrived at the theatre they went their separate ways, Bell to talk with the staff and workers, Holmes to the dressing room of Diana Strickland.

He knocked lightly upon the closed door.

'Come in, Sherlock,' a very feminine voice called from inside the room.

A thin smile played upon Holmes' lips as he slowly opened the door and entered the dressing room to behold a vision of loveliness that fairly took his breath away.

'You expected me?' Holmes said curiously.

'I am glad you are here without Joseph,' Diana said. 'I wanted to speak to you, to see you again, alone.'

Sherlock Holmes entered the dressing room, his eyes roving over Diana Strickland's face and form. She was seated at a dressing table before a large gilded gold mirror. She wore a white lace gown, her back towards him as she busily brushed her luxurious long red hair. She did it slowly and almost languidly, with long sensual motions the young man found most alluring.

Sherlock Holmes was entranced. He took a deep breath as Diana quickly turned around to face him. She allowed a luxurious smile to escape pouting red lips and the young man could not help but grin like an over-excited schoolboy at the sight of her. Diana was everything he had ever dreamed of or wanted in a woman. The young man stood there in awe, for once even forgetting the reason he had come to see her.

'You and Joseph talked to Rupert?' she asked softly.

'Yes, not an hour ago.'

'And I'm sure he told you all kinds of terrible things about me, Sherlock.'

'No, just that he has a different version of the story,' Holmes said, his eyes marvelling at Diana's alabaster skin, the swell of her breasts when she breathed and the bright allure of her deep blue eyes. A man could become lost in those eyes. He added softly, 'such is often the case when a husband and wife separate.'

'Come here, Sherlock,' she said, her voice light, her manner inviting. 'Sit down, beside me, and tell me what Joseph thinks.'

Holmes was only too happy to comply with her request and shared her settee in front of her dressing table. He felt his heart beat faster when he sat next to her. The closeness of their bodies produced a heat that seemed to grow between them.

'Your brother is most upset by this situation,' Holmes said, not knowing quite what to say now, or what was expected of him. 'He fears for your safety . . . as do I.'

'Oh, Sherlock, you are so sweet,' she said, then, adding, 'so he believes my story?'

'Entirely.'

Diana turned to look at Holmes, her lips pouting, her eyes looking into his own, 'And you, Sherlock, do you believe me?'

'Is it important to you that I do?'

'More than you can ever know,' she replied.

'Then yes, Diana, I believe you,' Holmes said looking into the deep blueness of her eyes, feeling the closeness of her beside him. Did he dare put his arm around her neck and draw those luscious lips down to his own? The heat was brewing inside him, passion boiling with fire. Sherlock Holmes was surprised by the feeling, shocked at how easy it would be for him to throw off all strictures of gentlemanly decorum and wallow in wild abandon. Diana gave him those feelings and he was both delighted and fearful of them.

As if reading his thoughts, Diana suddenly stood up and moved away from him, 'That's very nice to hear, Sherlock. But what do you and my brother intend to do about it all?'

Holmes' amorous plan evaporated as he watched her move away from him.

'Do about it?' he asked curiously.

'To protect me from that beast,' she said.

Holmes hadn't really thought things through that far ahead yet, and he cursed himself for a fool. He had to do something to meld Diana to him and so considered the question now. Apparently Strickland wouldn't try anything while he and Bell were here. However, once they left New York and went back to England,

Diana would once again be in danger. So the solution was simple; Diana must go back to England with them. Then she would be safely out of the range of her husband's violent rage and revenge. He told her this now.

Diana did not take it well at all. 'I don't think so, Sherlock,' she said sternly, even adamant. 'I am not going back to England. Maybe some day, but not now.'

'Well you can not stay in New York, it is much too dangerous for you here,' Holmes said. 'And we can not stay here and protect you indefinitely.'

Diana looked at him with a deep smile, 'Dear Sherlock, you do care about me, don't you?'

Holmes looked hurt, 'Of course, Diana.'

'Then you must convince Joseph to do something to help me.'

'Help you? How?'

'Protect me from Rupert,' she said softly. 'Make sure he can never hurt me again.'

For a moment a look of confusion came over the young man's face. What exactly was she asking of him? Moreover, it was not that he did not understand what her words entailed, but that such words should come from her of all people.

Then Diana walked over to him and slowly wrapped her arms around his neck as she brought his lips down to her own. It was everything Sherlock had ever dreamed it would be. They kissed long and passionately before she suddenly broke off the connection.

'Oh, my,' she said, 'I don't know what made me do that. I'm so sorry . . . '

'I'm not . . . ' Holmes replied quickly.

'Well, I just . . . oh Sherlock, I do feel a bond between us. Don't you feel it also? It is so strong, like a power over me. We should not deny these feelings.'

'Yes, Diana, I feel it too.'

Then she suddenly moved away from him again, 'Perhaps we should not become . . . involved? It may only complicate the situation.'

'No, Diana, you said so yourself we should not deny our feelings,' Holmes heard himself say out loud, though an inner voice told him he should say otherwise.

Diana smiled, 'Joseph will be here soon and I don't want him to see us like this. Come back later, tonight after my last show, in the alley by the stage door.'

Holmes looked up unable to hide his disappointment.

'Cheer up, Sherlock, dear,' she said with a promising wink, 'we shall have plenty of time together tonight. Remember, meet me at the stage door in the back alley, and bring flowers, Sherlock. A girl so does love to have a handsome beau bring her flowers. Now be gone, love.'

* * *

Sherlock Holmes walked out of Diana's dressing room and down the hall behind the stage in a delirious fog. Love and lust jousted within his mind and Diana was the prize. Long forgotten was the fact that she was a married woman, or that she was his friend and mentor's sister. Forgotten were the questions he had wanted to put to her after their earlier meeting with her husband.

Holmes looked for Doctor Bell but was

told by a stagehand that he had since left the theatre, so the young man walked back to his hotel alone, his mind a whirlwind of emotions he'd never quite felt before. Emotions he knew even less how to deal with. All he could do was count the hours until the end of Diana's stage show tonight, when he would see her again.

* * *

Bell wasn't in his room at the hotel when Holmes returned. The doctor came back a few hours later and the two men went out to one of New York's posh eateries for dinner and to compare notes.

Delmonicos had been famous in New York since 1825. The reputation was for fine and fashionable dining that seemed to rival the best that London had to offer. Formerly located in the Wall Street area the famous New York eatery had just opened up their new location on 14th Street and Fifth Avenue earlier that year. Holmes even considered making reservations to take Diana there one evening for a farewell dinner before they all returned to England but he did not mention that to Doctor Bell just then.

'So you spoke to my sister?' Bell asked his young assistant. 'How is she holding up?'

'Quite well, under the circumstances. She wants our help and is fearful that Strickland might try something soon,' Holmes said hiding the emotion in his voice.

'Aye, she's right to be concerned,' Bell said. Then he looked at his young companion and shook his head in exasperation. 'I just don't understand this, some things don't make sense to me.'

'I have also made certain inquiries today of the staff at that theatre. Not only the workers, but some of the actresses, the stage manager, they all told me the exact same story about that Rupert fellow.'

'That he's a dangerous man with a bad temper.'

'Yes, this was confirmed to me.'

'Quite so. Well, it follows the pattern

surely, just as Diana has told us,' Bell said.

'Of course,' Holmes said quietly, without much confidence.

'But something about it bothers you?' Bell asked.

'I don't know. I may be out of my depth in this type of thing and it may be more in league with your own methods, but it all seems a bit too perfect. I don't like this Rupert at all, and he certainly has a violent temper, but I have this nagging feeling it's all being rather masterfully contrived somehow.'

'You realize what you are implying?' Bell said surprised at Sherlock's words. 'Surely it must be as Diana says, evidence dictates as much.'

Holmes nodded quickly, 'Of course, doctor.'

'Sherlock?'

Holmes looked kindly at his friend trying to understand him.

'Your sister is lovely, talented and bright. I think she is an amazing woman. You are correct, we should do whatever we can to help her in her time of need,'

Holmes said with renewed energy, any doubt he had gone now.

'Quite right, Sherlock my boy, and well said,' Bell responded. Then with a twinkle in his eyes he looked closely at his young assistant and seemed to notice something for the first time. 'And I see she has worked some of her magic upon you as well.'

Sherlock Holmes blushed; Bell just smiled and laughed good-naturedly.

The two men continued their meal. The Chicago beefsteak was tender and delicious. When they finished the main course they relaxed over a delightful brandy and began to speak of future plans.

'Of course she can not be allowed to remain in New York,' Holmes stated.

'No,' Bell agreed. 'She must come back with us to England, or Edinburgh.'

'I broached that very subject to her earlier today and she made it quite clear to me that she does not wish to return to England any time soon. I am afraid she will not accompany us back home.'

Bell sighed, 'She was always a most

hard-headed girl and I'm sure that tendency has not lessened in her womanhood.'

'Then how do we convince her to leave with us?' Holmes asked, his mind already thinking about the pleasant journey home in Diana's company. 'She can not stay here in New York and we can not protect her every minute. I'm sure Strickland is staying his hand so long as we are here, but we can not remain in New York forever.'

'Yes,' Bell admitted. 'I fear that once we leave for home, Strickland will be free to act. Then he will surely murder my poor sister.'

Sherlock Holmes nodded, his face dark and gloomy. 'We must convince her to leave New York.'

'Perhaps I can speak some sense to her,' Bell offered, but his words held little confidence. He knew his sister well, so he did not have any great expectation of success.

* * *

That evening Diana was busy at the theatre so Bell stayed in his room working through an American medical journal. Holmes had begged off his companionship, saying he was going out for the evening to see a show.

'At the Criterion?' Bell asked with a sly wink.

Holmes didn't reply but the blush that came to his young face told the older man all he needed to know. 'Do tell Diana I said hello, Sherlock. And Sherlock?'

'Yes?'

'My sister is quite the alluring creature, but I would not allow myself to become inordinately enamored of her charms.'

* * *

On the way over to the Criterion the young man purchased a bundle of flowers from one of the numerous street hawkers. One dozen red roses would surely help pave the way to Diana's heart. His walk to the theatre was jaunty, light-hearted, the movements of a young man in love.

That night the Criterion was bright and

gay with many lights and colorful banners. The entrance was crowded with milling gentlemen in fine dress exiting the theatre. Sherlock Holmes quickly walked into the side alley. At the end a stage door was opened with the light from inside illuminating the area.

The young assistant to Dr. Bell was surprised to find that the alley was not at all empty of people at this late hour. In fact, there was a small group of half a dozen well-dressed men there, each carrying a bundle of flowers as was he.

As Sherlock Holmes drew closer to the group he looked over the men more closely. Some were older, others young, but all were obviously well-off or from wealthy families. All were also impeccably dressed. He watched as they met various young ladies from the theatre who until recently had performed upon the Criterion stage.

The women came out talking excitedly and were dressed for a lively evening on the town. Each accompanied one of the waiting men, and both were soon away. It all happened so quickly, it was all so pre-conceived and planned that a moment later Holmes found himself alone.

'Hey johnnyboy? Who you waiting 'round for?'

Holmes thought he had been alone but now saw a boy sitting upon a crate, the stage door boy on duty, no doubt.

'What did you call me?' Holmes asked sharply, he knew very well he had been the butt of some unsavory American slag and he did not like the sound of it at all.

'I called you Johnny,' the youth replied boldly with a derisive laugh. 'Just another stage-door Johnny come to see the gals. Well, who you waiting for? They're all gone by now and I think you're plum outta luck.'

'Diana Strickland,' Holmes said.

'Oh, the Princess Herself!' the boy laughed knowingly. 'You'll not win the likes of her with just flowers . . . '

'Impertinent wretch!' Holmes growled at the boy.

The youth only laughed, 'She's long gone, Mister, off with her Professor friend.'

Sherlock Holmes looked back at the

boy, 'She's not . . . here?'

'Gone an hour ago, saw her myself.'

'I was to meet her here, we had an appointment after the show,' Holmes said softly, more to himself than to the boy. Suddenly his face flushed with heat and he felt like a fool. The red roses he held so proudly in his arms had now become a flag to that foolishness.

'You have a girl, young fellow?' Holmes asked the boy.

'I sure do,' he answered boldly. 'Clarissa Wells on Warren Street.'

'Good,' Holmes handed off the bundle of roses to the boy, 'then give these to her.'

Before the boy could utter a word the bundle of flowers was thrust upon him and the well-dressed young gentleman was out of the alley and gone.

⋆ ⋆ ⋆

That night Sherlock Holmes walked the lonely streets of New York alone. His mind full of conflicting thoughts that made for ill company indeed. His emotions were raw, his passion had been stoked and his feelings were hurt. Why had she done this to him? Arranged a meeting and then gone off with another man! He felt terrible. The analytical part of his mind was truly amazed at the amount of pain this caused him. He wished he could talk to Mycroft about it, surely his more worldly older brother knew how to deal with such things.

'She must have forgotten our assignation,' Holmes heard himself say, grasping for any hope. He walked the dark lonely street slowly as if in a trance. 'Surely that must be it! Perhaps there was some kind of emergency or an important meeting with this professor? She forgot all about 'us', but I am sure she will be terribly upset and sorry when I remind her.'

And yet, something nagged deeply inside his young heart, a little voice that he could not stifle but so far had been able to explain itself to him.

* * *

'Where were you last night?' Bell asked when they met for breakfast the next morning. He knew his young assistant had been out almost all night. 'You had me worried. I have heard this city can be quite dangerous after dark.'

'I was out walking,' Holmes replied guardedly.

'All night?'

'I was thinking,' Holmes replied and Bell could feel the pain in his young companion's voice and so did not press him.

'I also was doing some thinking, Sherlock,' Bell admitted, changing the subject now. 'In fact, I did quite a bit more. I went around to my sister's room at Mrs. Shay's quite early this morning to speak to her. You'll never guess what I saw there.'

'The Professor?' Holmes blurted.

'The Professor? No, no professor, it was Strickland.'

'Really?' Holmes said surprised now in spite of his dark mood.

'For a couple whose relationship has been complicated with accusations of attempted murder, they seemed to be quite fond of each other. I watched as

Diana kissed Rupert goodbye, I heard her tell him she loved him dearly.'

A dark cloud covered young Sherlock's face, he did not verbally respond to this news, he could not respond. Bell noted his companion's dark look.

'My feelings exactly,' Bell stated. 'Something is not right here.'

Holmes nodded, 'I think we need to speak to Strickland and get the truth out of him.'

Bell was about to reply when there was a loud knocking upon the door. Bell answered to find a hotel bellboy framed in the doorway and behind him another boy in working clothes. Holmes recognized that boy at once as being from the Criterion.

The bellboy moved out of the way and the other boy said, 'Begging your pardon, sir, but are you Doctor Bell?'

'Yes, I am Bell,' the doctor said impatiently.

'Well, I was sent by Mr. Jacobs of the Criterion. He said to fetch you at once. A terrible accident has happened. There has been a killing.'

Bell looked at Holmes frantically, each fearing to utter what was uppermost in their thoughts. Bell quickly blurted, 'Do you know who it was?'

'No, sir,' the boy replied nervously.

'Well was it a woman?' Holmes asked sharply.

'Don't know sir, I wasn't there. Mr. Jacobs told me to run and fetch you immediately. All I know is that it happened in Mrs. Strickland's dressing room.'

Bell let out a muffled curse, 'My God, he's finally done it, Sherlock!'

Holmes said not one word but his soul was drowning in a sea of dark desperation.

⋆ ⋆ ⋆

Bell and Holmes rushed to the Criterion where they were met by Mr. Jacobs, the Director, who quickly led them into the back of the theatre to Diana Strickland's dressing room.

'It's terrible, doctor,' Jacobs said as Bell, Holmes and he ran through the backstage area. All was chaos and police were everywhere. 'I knew you would want to be called immediately.'

Bell nodded, a dark gloom covering his face at the director's dire words as he and Holmes turned the corner and frantically entered Diana's dressing room.

There upon the floor lay Rupert Strickland, a bullet hole in his chest. He was obviously dead. Diana Strickland was crying at her dressing table, surrounded by two men who looked to be New York Police detectives.

Doctor Bell heaved a sigh of relief when he saw that his sister was alive. He then went to Strickland; after a quick examination he pronounced him dead. Meanwhile Holmes immediately ran to Diana's side trying to comfort her. He felt crushing pain when he realized she hardly noticed his presence at all. Two detectives were finishing with their questions.

'Diana!' Holmes cried out trying to get her attention, but she still ignored him.

'Oh Joseph, help me!' she cried once she saw her brother.

'What happened here?' Bell asked

frantic. Brother and sister embraced for a long moment. She was still sobbing when they parted, then she saw Holmes and quickly embraced him as well, 'Oh, Sherlock.'

'What happened, Diana?' Sherlock asked quickly.

'Oh, it was terrible. It's all my fault, I'm afraid, I made a terrible mistake,' she cried.

The older detective said that he was satisfied with Diana's explanation of the events, then asked who the newcomers were. She told them. The detective nodded, said she might be asked some more questions before a magistrate later, but that the witnesses all backed up her story so she was free to go.

'Thank you,' Diana stammered as the two detectives left the room.

Bell and Holmes stood by frantic to hear an explanation.

'Oh, Joseph, it was terrible. Sherlock, you must not think badly of me,' she stammered, crying again now. Bell tried to calm her. Sherlock brought her a glass of water from a nearby pitcher. She drank thankfully, quickly, then seemed to regain her composure.

'Tell me what happened here,' Bell insisted.

Diana nodded, took a deep breath to summon her wits. 'How everything could turn so wrong I cannot fathom. Rupert contacted me through a friend of his, a visiting professor, who had convinced him that he should attempt to reconcile. It was the Professor who came to see me last night and convinced me to see Rupert. Sherlock, I know you were disappointed but I hope you understand that I had to take this one last chance to save my marriage. Rupert is my husband. I know he loves me and I . . . thought I loved him. The Professor brought me to see Rupert and we met at a neutral location, a well-known restaurant, called Delmonico's.'

Holmes felt a twinge somewhere deep inside him.

'You met Rupert alone? Was that wise?' Bell asked.

'Maybe not but we sat together, we ate and talked and after a while it was like all the trouble between us had been set aside and ended. We made up, you see. Finally, Joseph, things looked bright after so much darkness. Rupert came with me to my room, Mrs. Shay would never have allowed it had she known, but we were discreet. We are married after all . . . and he stayed the night with me. It was like a . . . second honeymoon.'

Bell nodded, Holmes remained quiet, outwardly stoic but the knowledge was tearing him apart inside.

'I really thought we were going to be together again and that all was finally well between us. I sent him off this morning with nothing but love in my heart,' Diana said.

Bell turned to Holmes and caught his eye, any suspicions he had were gone now that he understood what he had seen early that morning outside Mrs. Shay's.

Then Diana began again, 'But it all turned so bad so quickly, Joseph. It was his jealously. Rupert's anger and violence could not be contained. He came here demanding I leave the theatre again. I told him we could talk about it later, he would hear nothing of it. We argued . . . he hit me.'

Bell raged when he noticed for the first time new bruises on his sister's arms and neck. Holmes had noticed these straight away but had said nothing though inwardly seething. He thought about how quickly Rupert's temper had flared when they had met him earlier that day.

'He hurt me, Joseph,' she added, the pain she showed in her face was mirrored in the face of Bell and Holmes. 'Then he took out a gun and pointed it at me. He told me he'd rather I was dead than have to share me with other men when I was upon the stage. Some of the stagehands rushed in, attracted by the shouting no doubt. They pushed Rupert from behind, he dropped the gun. It slid over to me and I picked it up and pointed it at him. I told him to stay away, pleaded with him to leave me alone, but he just kept walking toward me with that bestial look in his eyes. His arms reached out for my neck. He was going to kill me, strangle me right there, I was sure of it. I don't think he believed I could pull the trigger, neither did I, but when I looked into the cold blackness of his eyes I knew I had no choice. It all happened so quickly. I pulled the trigger and sent the bullet that killed him into his heart.'

They were all quiet for a moment.

'Who are these witnesses?' Holmes asked carefully.

'Two stage hands, and the Professor was here. They saw it all and will back up my story,' Diana said confidently.

There didn't seem to be much else to say or do. Holmes went to speak to the stagehands and they corroborated Diana's story. They seemed credible. He couldn't find the Professor; the man had apparently left right after speaking to the police. However since he also corroborated Diana's story, there seemed no pressing need to locate him.

The affair, as far as the police were concerned was at an end, and Bell and Holmes had to admit they were much relieved that Rupert was no longer a threat to Diana. At least now, Diana would be safe and this entire affair was done with.

* * *

'She would never have come home with us,' Bell told Holmes once they were back at their hotel that night after leaving Diana at Mrs. Shay's. She seemed to be doing rather well under the circumstances but wanted to be alone and they respected her wishes.

Bell had tickets on the *Oceanic* for her return voyage, which was leaving the next morning to Liverpool and England. Luck and good timing allowed them to take advantage of those tickets, rather than wait weeks for another return voyage. Of course that gave them no time to spend with Diana but both men were relieved the affair was over and now she would be safe.

'At least it all worked out for the best,' Bell said as he packed his valise.

Holmes nodded absently. 'I am much relieved your sister is safe. However, I find it interesting that while Diana has killed her husband, albeit in self-defense, she now stands to inherit all of his substantial wealth. I find that incredibly ironic.'

Bell nodded, 'Ironic or not, Sherlock, I am just thankful that beast is dead and Diana is alive. Now we can go home with a clean conscience and the knowledge of a successful journey. I fear I've taken you away from your scientific studies for far too long.'

'Not at all,' Holmes said with a quick nod of his head. 'This entire affair has been most instructive and enlightening. In fact, it has peaked my interest in criminal investigation considerably; so much so that I now believe such a career to be my one true calling.'

* * *

The violin was played fast and furious, loud with frenzied improvisation; it spoke from behind the solid oak door with a fierce burning passion. The sound stopped with his first knock, then she let him in.

'I knew you'd come,' she said simply.

'I had no idea you played the violin,' he began, watching her as she put the instrument down and then came over to him. 'I have often thought of taking it up myself some day.'

'You really should, Sherlock. I find it very conducive to the thinking process, and it can be quite relaxing,' she said with a smile, taking his hand in hers. She led him to a settee in the corner of her room at Mrs. Shay's.

'We leave first thing tomorrow morning and I had to see you one last time,' he said softly, trying to hide the ardor in his voice.

They sat down. She offered him tea. He declined with a wave of his hand. She said nothing else, but just looked at him.

'What will happen now?' he asked.

'You and Joseph will go back home and I shall continue my stage career here in New York,' she said simply.

'I don't mean that,' he said. 'I mean between us?'

'Sherlock, please don't make this more difficult for me than it is. I've been through so much with Rupert. I really do like you. You're smart and good and any woman would be lucky to have you. I know some day if you apply yourself you will do quite well in whatever career you choose. I'm sure.'

The words hurt him savagely, though he was sure they were not meant to do so. Such was the way of love he had finally learned. It told him the door to her heart was closed tight, forever. It was almost too terrible to accept.

'How much was Rupert Strickland worth?' he said taking a different tack.

'I don't know for certain, millions of dollars, pounds even. He had substantial properties back home, gold mines in South Africa, too much to even think about now,' she replied.

'Now it's all yours,' he said. It was a statement, not a question.

'Yes, Rupert was the sole heir,' she explained. 'As his wife I stand to inherit all his holdings. Oh, there are some other family members, cousins, a dowager aunt, all well-off in their own right, but none stand to inherit from Rupert's demise.'

'Demise?' Holmes said curiously. 'That's an odd way to put it. You killed him.'

She bristled, recovered quickly, then replied, 'I had no choice.'

'I'm sorry, 'killed' was a poor choice of

words on my part,' Holmes said and saw the relief in her eyes. 'What I meant to say was that you murdered him.'

Diana's eyes shot wide for an instant, anger, rage even, but there was no fear. Then her face softened and she looked longingly at him, 'Oh, Sherlock, how can you be so cruel. Don't you want me to be happy after all I have been through?'

'Tell me about the Professor?'

'There's nothing to tell,' she said.

'What is his part in this?'

Diana's face clouded, her lips pursed for a moment but she did not speak right away. Holmes knew she was deciding what to tell him, working it out in her mind, trying to gauge her response by determining just how much he knew. She laughed lightly, gaily, 'I met him last year when he came here to lecture, now he has returned and we have resumed our friendship.'

'And you love him?'

She nodded, then boldly added, 'Yes, I do love him and he loves me. You have no idea of the power of his mind and personality, what he can accomplish. He is a brilliant man.'

'I could be brilliant for you, Diana,' Holmes heard himself say. 'If you would only let me.'

Diana smiled, apparently touched by the young man's words. And while Holmes saw not a hint of mockery in her response, he saw no love there for him either. Then she looked away, hiding her face from him. He could not tell if she was crying . . . or laughing.

Young Sherlock bowed his head in sadness.

'I'm afraid it's all done, Sherlock,' she said with a definiteness that brooked no argument. 'Go back home with my brother. Learn from him. He is a brilliant man, in his own way. I do hope you find in your life all that you seek and truly need.'

'As long as your brother doesn't realize?' Holmes countered.

'Realize what?' she asked carefully.

Holmes smiled grimly, 'You know.'

'Sherlock, my love, why do you doubt my word?'

'It bothers me that you claim there

were three men who came into your dressing room when Rupert pulled the gun out. You said they knocked the gun from his hand, yet three men could not restrain him from attacking you? Come now! Tell me the truth.'

Diana merely smiled, shrugged, 'About all this, the plan to steal the Strickland millions? Oh, don't look so shocked now, Sherlock, I have no worry about admitting it to you. You're nobody of consequence. I do not care now. I can tell you all if I so desire. I know you suspected as much.'

'Yes, but I simply could not believe it of *you*,' he said softly, rather sadly.

She smiled victorious, 'That is because you did not *want* to believe it, Sherlock. And I counted on that.'

He nodded, inwardly hurt but angry now — with her and himself.

'I can read you, Sherlock, I can read you like a book. It does not matter now. I can freely admit it before you and there is nothing you or anyone else can do about it. If you bring it to the authorities, I shall deny everything. You have no proof, while

I have witnesses. No one can change the outcome. Not now.'

'Tell me the truth then. What happened in your dressing room?'

'Silly boy, I'm afraid I played poor Rupert from the very beginning. His family tried to warn him but his passion bound him to me, and when the time was right — when you and my brother arrived — I struck. See, you two were the final pieces to this puzzle. Rupert thought we were finally to reconcile. We did. The Professor and his men brought him to me, and I shot him dead. You should have seen the surprise on poor Rupert's face!' She laughed at the memory of his murder.

Holmes said nothing, his mind a cauldron of conflicting emotions.

'Oh, Sherlock, don't look so shocked. You really were out of your league here. I played you and my brother just as I played poor Rupert. It was so easy. I sent for Joseph because I knew being the dear brother he is, that he would validate my story. And if anything went wrong, he was my insurance. You see, his being such an eminent doctor and all could prove useful, I would convince him to plead my case, perhaps even fake the proper documents. However, none of that proved necessary. It is over now. Much like you, Joseph could never believe anything evil of me, the dear man — the dear fool! And you, Sherlock? Why you are just another, far lesser and insignificant dupe! You thought to win my affections — ' she laughed bitterly and her vile reaction cut him like a knife — 'I have a far better man than you could ever be. A man who understands me completely unto the very depth of my soul.'

'If you have one,' Holmes countered harshly.

'Oh bitter boy! You are just like all men, wanting what you cannot have, and angry when you can not have it!' she replied laughing wildly. 'You were used, Sherlock Holmes! Admit it, I played your emotions like I played that violin!'

Holmes was shocked by the length and breadth of her boldness, of her evil.

'And I know you will not say one word to anyone about it — especially not dear brother, Joseph. I've seen the way you look at him, how you admire, even worship him,' Diana said full of confidence. 'Should you ever tell him the truth about me and what I have done, I am sure he would never believe you.'

Holmes remained quiet, thoughtful, a small but growing part of him was analyzing her words carefully and finding the entire situation most instructive, even as he felt a pain and hurt he had never experienced before.

'And if he somehow did believe you,' she added, 'I can assure you the news would kill him. Then you would murder poor Joseph as clearly as I murdered poor Rupert.'

Holmes let her words flow over him.

She smiled demurely, 'You see, Joseph is a good and loving brother and I knew he would be all for me, and then welcome me when I came back home to claim my fortune.'

'You plan to return to England?' Holmes asked.

'Some day, the professor and I will return to take charge of the Strickland holdings,' she said simply. 'He has some ideas about developing a certain organization and the Strickland wealth will prove most useful in that endeavour.'

'How could you, Diana!' Sherlock Holmes voiced his feelings of moral outrage in full bloom.

Diana Strickland began to laugh uncontrollably at his words, their clear morality wrenching her with hysterical mirth. 'Oh, callow youth of but 22 years, you are priceless! Now, Sherlock, you must take your leave of me. Hurry now! For my own true love will be here soon. Do have a safe journey back to England.'

She had dismissed him, such as one does a lowly servant, or child.

Holmes stood his ground, 'I have just one last question to ask you and would like an answer.'

Diana smiled sweetly, waiting.

'Where did the bruises and welts come from? They were real enough, I know. Were they self-inflicted?'

'Oh, those? No, they were not self-inflicted, nor were they from Rupert,' she giggled, licking her lips. 'You see, my professor friend's ardor tends to extremes.

Sometimes he gets carried away by his passion, sometimes I do as well.'

Holmes looked down sadly.

'Oh, Sherlock, don't stand there and feel sorry for yourself,' she chided.

Holmes looked up boldly, 'The one I feel sorry for, Diana, is yourself. Good-bye.'

* * *

The sea journey back to Liverpool and England was upon rough and gloomy seas. The hearty companionship between Holmes and Bell had fallen upon similar circumstances. Young Holmes had much on his mind. He had grown to admire Doctor Bell and was proud to call him a friend. He knew he had to tell him the dark truth about his sister but he feared the impact it would have on their friendship. What was he to do?

And with that the American adventure of Dr. Joseph Bell and Sherlock Holmes came to a close, even as it continued to have repercussions in both men's lives until their dying days.

Part V: Baker Street, October, 1911

Sherlock Holmes sighed, drew once more upon his pipe and looked up at Watson.

'Well, Holmes?' Watson blurted impatiently. 'You can't just stop there! What happened?'

'What do you think happened, old friend?'

Watson sat silent for a moment thinking it through. 'Oh my God, so you told him! You told Doctor Bell all about his sister and how she had planned the murder of her own husband?'

'Yes,' Holmes admitted. 'I had to. We were companions, friends, I admired him greatly. Still do, John. I loved that man like a brother. I could never keep the truth from him and still say I was his friend.'

Watson cleared his throat nervously, 'I imagine he did not take it well.'

'You are correct,' Holmes said softly, remembering. 'I told him that first night, when our ship left New York. He would not believe a word of it. He said it was all because I was infatuated with Diana, angry with her because she had spurned my advances. I tried to reason with him, John, make him see the logic of it, or at least consider what she herself had told me in her own words, but it was no use. It was terrible. I had told him that the sweet and lovely sister he worshipped lead a secret life of deceit, treachery, murder and evil. I told him his sister was a monster.'

Watson sighed, sad to see the pain on his friend's face.

'I pleaded with him, John,' Holmes recalled softly. 'How can you be so blind?' I told him. He replied 'Sherlock, how can you be so hard-headed and obstinate against her!'

Watson sat quietly taking it all in.

'You see, he and I could not agree on anything at this point,' Holmes added sadly, 'least of all about Diana. She was the one fixed point in both our universes back then. I finally threw up my hands and told him if I was proved right about her I would rather keep bees and watch birds in Sussex than ever hurt his feelings. He told me that would be a far better career path than the one I had chosen because I was allowing emotion to blur the facts. I accused him of the very same error. I cannot in good conscience blame him. He loved Diana — as did I — and she had made her plans well. After that, he would not listen and refused to hear another word and there was not much else to say.'

'Oh, Holmes.'

'The next day Doctor Bell had the Captain move me and my belongings to another stateroom. Joseph never spoke another word to me again.'

'Oh, God, Holmes, I am so sorry. It must have been terrible for you, and all these long years you two never spoke?'

'Never again, and now he's gone,' Holmes said, his face soft and sad. 'So much left unsaid. Never a chance for a real goodbye before he passed.'

Watson watched his old friend and felt his great sadness and loss. It was a loss that he knew now was compounded by decades of missed opportunities and lost friendship.

'What of this Professor you mentioned?' Watson asked gently, trying to change the subject. 'I'm almost afraid to ask you if it was . . . '

'It was he,' Holmes replied bitterly, not wanting to even mention the man's name.

Watson shook his head in shock, it was almost too much to take in at once. He had known Holmes, been his closest confidant and friend for decades, and now to learn of all this pain and hurt from so early in his life — he felt sorry for him carrying it around inside for so long. Holmes had been such a young man when he had found and lost his true love, learned the evil truth of her, and the truth of her evil. On top of all that he had lost all relations with his best friend and mentor. It was a bitter pill to swallow at so young an age.

Watson also saw another piece of the puzzle that made up the complex persona of his friend. For he now realized that this American adventure seemed to cement Holmes's view of the female sex long before ever Irene Adler came upon the scene — another lovely and talented adventuress who reminded Holmes of Diana Strickland, no doubt.

'And now he's gone,' Holmes said softly.

John Watson hardly knew what to say.

'Doctor Bell was the wisest and most noble man I ever knew,' Holmes said, then with a wry smile he added, 'aside from one John H. Watson, of course.'

'Why, thank you, Holmes,' Watson stammered, truly touched by his friend's gracious words.

'Now they're all gone,' Holmes reminisced. 'Bell was the last one. Moriarty was the first to go, aided by my own hand. Diana committed suicide shortly after the Professor went over the Falls. Had I but known . . . He never married her, but she remained loyal and steadfast by his side all her life, his mistress to the end. Her inheritance formed the financial source for his criminal empire.'

'It is an amazing and tragic story, Holmes,' Watson said softly. 'So that is how it all ends. What happens now?'

Sherlock Holmes gave a rueful smile as he took something out of the pocket of his robe.

'I say, Holmes, What have you there? A letter?'

'Would you be a good fellow, John, and read it out loud.'

Holmes handed the mysterious envelope to his friend, who took it in hand most carefully.

'I was given it by Mrs. Abernathy, the charwoman, when I went up North last week to close Dr. Bell's house,' Holmes explained. 'I have held it unopened since then.'

Watson looked astonished, 'But how could you not read it immediately? If it were I, I should . . . '

Holmes nodded, 'I know, but I feared the moment I would open it and what I might find written therein. When I met with Mrs. Abernathy she said she knew that I would come. Bell had instructed her to wait for me.'

'Really?' Watson said in surprise.

'Yes, and when I asked her what his mood had been when he wrote the letter, she told me it had not been good at all. She said, 'I don't know, Mr. Holmes, but the doctor was in a foul mood when he gave me the envelope with his instructions to give it to you upon his death'.'

Watson examined the envelope, noting the quality of the paper as he looked at the address written upon it. 'It's addressed to you, 'Sherlock Holmes, 221b Baker Street, London' and the return address is 'Dr. Joseph Bell, Edinburgh, Scotland'.'

'Open it, John,' Holmes said. 'I believe it is time.'

Watson nodded, then slit open the envelope with Holmes' own dagger and then withdrew the contents. There was just one sheet of folded bond writing paper, which he unfolded nervously.

'Well, read it,' Holmes prompted him impatiently.

'Of course,' Watson replied. After clearing his throat he began:

''Dear Sherlock, I am quite cross as I write this letter, but not with you old friend, but with my own self. We have been at odds and loath to speak these past forty years, the fault of which I put squarely upon my own shoulders. I acted abominably to you and I hope you can forgive me.

Emotions not only skew judgment they can ruin friendships. I want you to know I have never had you far from my thoughts. The truth is I have followed your career, every case, all these many years with great interest and much satisfaction. I have rejoiced with your every success, particularly against that evil fellow who so deservedly went over the falls. My only regret in that matter, as I know you agree, was the result it inflicted upon my sister, Diana.

There, I have mentioned her name. No longer should her evil deeds be a barrier between us. I tell you now that you were correct about her all along. It is sometimes difficult for an old Scot to admit the errors of his ways. We tend to carry those mistakes with us too long in life and even unto the grave.

Sherlock, I am proud of the man you have become. I am proud to have known you and call you friend, I remember with great fondness our American adventure. I have followed your life and career, albeit from afar, and tell you now in all honesty and profound respect: well done, Sherlock Holmes! Very well done indeed'!'

Watson saw a great softness come to the face of Sherlock Holmes. One lone tear, then another, made their way down his cheek but when he saw Holmes look at him and smile he sighed with relief, knowing that what he had seen were not tears of sadness, but tears of joy.

Watson wiped a tear from his own eye. There was a long silence.

'It is of course signed, 'I remain your most devoted servant, Dr. Joseph Bell, Edinburgh',' Watson added softly with a noticeable tightening in his voice and a lump in his throat.

'Well now, my friend,' Holmes continued looking much relieved, 'I feared what that letter might say, but since Joseph and I can finally agree on Diana now, maybe I can still keep that oath made to him and end my days as a consulting detective. You see, I really do have a desire to roam the Sussex downs, enjoying nothing more taxing than keeping bees and watching birds after so many years of grim work.'

'Really, Holmes!' Watson exclaimed sharply. 'I don't believe that for a minute.'

The Great Detective did not reply.

'Holmes?' Watson prompted. 'Can you tell me what inscription you placed upon his monument?'

'A quote from the *Bible*, Dan X. II. Do you know it?'

'I'm sorry to say that I do not.'

Sherlock Holmes smiled warmly and said, 'Well it is quite simple really. I have found that the shortest phrase often has the deepest meaning. Four words say it all quite well, my friend:

''*A Man Greatly Beloved*'.'

THE END

Other titles in the
Linford Mystery Library:

THE ATLANTIC TUNNEL

John Russell Fearn

Deep beneath the floor of the Atlantic Ocean, scientists and engineers attempt the most daring and audacious scientific project of all time: the construction of an undersea tunnel between Great Britain and Canada; linking Land's End with Labrador. Canadian and British teams work simultaneously at either end, to converge in the middle. Using scientific methods to fight the crushing pressure and geological and marine perils involved, the brave workers face a far greater hazard — the danger within — from saboteurs!

PAY BACK

Norman Lazenby

Rick Manton and Thelma Wain were two young people in love — but they were also grifters, who recognised no moral code and considered themselves above the law. And when mobster Dan Sweder moved to take over the drug traffic in Los Angeles, they found their own small dope dealing operation was being squeezed out. Rick and Thelma had only one answer: Dan Sweder had to die! So they set out to 'eliminate' him — two small-time crooks against the Mob!

FIVE FORGOTTEN STORIES

John Hall

In the winter of 1934–1935, according to H.P. Lovecraft's *The Haunter of the Dark*, Robert Blake had settled down alone, to work . . . He had painted 'nameless, unhuman monsters', and 'profoundly alien, non-terrestrial landscapes' — and also, we are told, written five short stories, later believed lost. However, an exercise book, which belonged to a certain 'Robert Blake' of Providence, has been recently acquired — the contents, when deciphered, appear to be five weird tales . . .

THE LUCK MACHINE

E. C. Tubb

The world is surrounded by intangible energies of which man has little knowledge. Electricity, once an unsuspected natural force, is now a known reality . . . so why not luck? Once recognised as an actual force, the next step is to construct a machine to harness its forces. However, if one person attracts good luck, another is due for bad luck. And when the Luck Machine falls into the wrong hands, the inventors wish they'd stuck to rabbits' feet and black cats . . .